# THE SEVENTH SERGEANT

## THREE RIVERS RANCH ROMANCE: BOOK SIX

### LIZ ISAACSON

AEJ CREATIVE WORKS

ISBN-13: 978-1537728735

ISBN-10: 1537728733

"O love the Lord, all ye his saints: for the Lord preserveth the faithful, and plentifully rewardeth the proud doer."

— PSALMS 31:23

The sky surrounding Carly Watters had never seemed so wide, so blue, so threatening. Of course, she hadn't set foot outside the city in half a decade. Her heart pulsed out an extra beat as she made a right turn and faced yet another two-lane highway without a single soul in sight.

The previous veteran care handler had told her Three Rivers Ranch was another forty minutes north of town. Carly had half-thought she'd been kidding. But now, with her orchid satin heels pressing against the accelerator and the minutes ticking by, she realized Lex hadn't exaggerated at all.

Dismay tore through her when her tires met dirt instead of asphalt, and she knew her shoes wouldn't survive more than a couple of steps in the dust and gravel. She'd bought the heels as a graduation gift for herself when she'd finished her social work Master's degree at TCU a couple of years ago, and they remained the most expensive piece of her wardrobe.

"This is a good job," she breathed to herself as that wide-open sky continued to suffocate her. "It's a promotion—one where you can afford to buy another pair of three hundred dollar shoes. So what if you have to come out to the sticks every couple of weeks? It's going to be fine."

But as she pulled her cute, compact car into the parking lot next to a newer building, a sinking sensation in her stomach spoke that nothing would be fine. Carly pulled up the zipper on her jacket and reached for the file of the veteran she'd come all the way out to this ranch to see: Reese Sanders.

A Sergeant, Reese had suffered massive core injuries from a bombing a few years ago. Carly had already pored over Lex's notes, and she expected to find a "happy-go-lucky veteran who left his wheelchair behind after endless hours of horseback riding."

After she'd read his file, Carly had admired his tenacity, the way he'd clawed himself back from the edge of physical devastation. She'd had a hint of that kind of heartache in her life too, but it tasted bitter in the back of her throat and she painted over it with a fresh layer of lipstick and a smile almost as bright as the near-spring sun.

One of her mother's adages sprang to her mind. *Comparison is the thief of joy.*

Carly had tried to make the words mean something in her life, but with two Mary Poppins Practically Perfect in Every Way older sisters, and a twin sister that Carly was technically older than, she'd never quite been able to measure up.

Even her choice of social work—of dedicating her life to helping others—had been overshadowed by her twin's acceptance into a Ph.D program.

She locked her car as she clicked across the blessedly paved parking lot, the familiar *ba-beep!* somehow strengthening her to carry out this meeting in her usual cheerful manner. The wind caught her hair and blew the blonde locks around her face. She scrambled for the door handle, the weather pulling at her skirt, her jacket, her file.

Almost like God had pressed the fast-forward button on her

life, the wind ripped the folder from Carly's grip. The folder containing all of Reese's accomplishments. The folder the previous handler had warned her not to misplace or rearrange. The folder that symbolized the beginning of her new career.

The weather snatched at the pages, sent them twirling through the air, and Carly could do nothing but watch. All at once, her life resumed its normal pace—all except her pulse, which thundered at four times its normal speed. She swiped for the pages with her hands, stomped on others with her precious heels, even hipped one into the doorjamb to keep it from getting sucked into the open Texas range, never to be seen again.

As she attempted to gather together what pages she could, the crunching of paper behind her attracted her attention. She turned, hoping for a handsome cowboy with exceptional lassoing skills.

She got the handsome cowboy bit about right, and she straightened, forgetting about the need to keep her hip curved into the building.

"Let me help you." He bent to grab a fistful of papers before they could be tornadoed away. When he straightened, his dark eyes sparkled with a smile, causing Carly's chest to squeeze in a good way.

"That must be your purple car." He nodded his cowboy-hatted head toward the parking lot.

Her defenses rose. "I like purple."

The man drank in her orchid heels. "Obviously."

"It gets good gas mileage."

"I'm sure it does." He took a couple of stunted steps forward, his hand outstretched, and understanding flooded her. "I'm Reese Sanders. What can I help you with?"

Instead of answering, she reached for his hand and catalogued the thrill that squirreled down her spine at the contact. Warmth from his skin bled into hers, and she allowed her lips to curve upward. "I'm looking for you, Sergeant Sanders." With a measure of regret she didn't quite understand, she withdrew her fingers from his. "I'm your new veteran care coordinator, Carly Watters."

"Ah." He glanced down at the papers again before pushing them toward her. "These must be Lex's notes." Reese shuffled backward, and it looked like he might fall. Carly automatically reached out to steady him.

The death glare he gave first to her hand on his forearm and then which he speared straight into her eyes left zero doubt about how he felt. She yanked her hand back, heat rising through her chest to her cheeks.

"S-sorry," she mumbled, her pinpoint heels suddenly too small to hold her weight. She sagged into the building again, not caring that it slouched her figure, despite her mother's warning voice in her head. "Can we go in? You were expecting me, right? Lex told me—"

"I've been expectin' you, yeah." He bent and collected a paper stuck against the glass, handed it to her, and entered the building before holding the door open for her. "We can meet in the conference room." He nodded to the right. "Through there."

Carly took a deep breath as she passed him, not because she wanted to get a better sense of his smoky, spicy scent, but because she needed the extra oxygen to settle her nerves. Hadn't she read in that blasted file that Reese resisted help? That the only reason he'd even signed up for services was because someone else had called first?

Once inside the conference room, Carly shoved the papers back into the folder, intending to sort through them and put them back in order when she could be alone. She didn't need him to witness first-hand her OCD when it came to her client's files. She moved to the head of the table and sat down.

"So," she started. "Tell me about your job here."

Reese closed the door and moved to the chair next to hers. He possessed a fluidity in his injury, something Carly hadn't expected. She admired the dark stubble along his jaw and found herself fantasizing about what it would feel like against her cheek. If his lips would be soft in comparison as they touched hers.

Her hand flew to her mouth as she sucked in a breath. She needed to find her center, stop this ridiculous train of crazy thoughts. Reese was a *client*. A veteran she was supposed to help. Nothing more.

"I'm the receptionist here at Courage Reins." Reese spoke with quiet authority, and another traitorous trickle of delight made her skin prickle.

"I answer phones, make appointments, help with the horses. That kind of stuff."

Carly pulled out a random piece of paper from the folder and flipped it over. She clicked her pen into operational mode and wrote something. What, she didn't even know. She just wanted to look official, like she knew what she was doing. "You live in Three Rivers?"

"Yeah."

"You drive out here everyday?"

"Everyday I want to get paid."

Carly glanced up from her chicken scratch at the gruff amusement in his voice. His dark diamond eyes studied her, unsettling her and making her next question abandon her mind. Heat rumbled through her stomach, rising until it settled in her face. She shoved the useless notes back into the folder. "What can I help you with, Sergeant Sanders?"

He leaned away from the table, his injury nowhere near his impressive biceps. The biceps that bulged as he crossed his arms and continued watching her with those gorgeous eyes. He seemed to be able to see right through her pretended professionalism.

"I don't need help," he said. "I'm doin' great. That's what I told Lex a month ago, when she said she was leavin'."

"It's procedure when a new care coordinator—"

Reese lifted one hand, rendering her silent. "I know," he said. "I get it. But I don't need anything right now. I'm good."

Oh, he was. Carly licked her lips and pressed them together, a slim vein of frustration sliding through her. She'd driven two hours for him to tell her he was good?

"Well, maybe I can get some groceries for you on my way back through town."

"I do all my shopping online."

Her eyebrows shot up. "You do your grocery shopping online?"

"You say that like I don't know how to use a computer." A deep chuckle accompanied the words. "It's easy, Miss Carly. You just login to this app, order what you want, and show up at the store. They bring everything right to me. I don't even get out of my truck."

Of course he'd drive a truck. Probably one of those huge, obnoxious pick-ups that she could never see around. Still, she wanted to hear him say *Miss Carly* over and over.

She cleared her throat and straightened the already-straight file. "You sure there's nothing you need? I could stick something in the oven, start a sprinkler, get your mail—"

His arms uncrossed and his left hand came down on hers. "Miss Carly, I don't need anything. But if you wanted to hang around here for a while, I could show you the horses."

Panic streamed through her, mixing with a wild thread of joy at his touch. She could hardly sort through how to feel, not to mention what to say.

Finally, her mind came up with *He needs company*. And she could give him that, if nothing else.

"I—Okay," she said. "But I don't think I've ever seen a horse up close."

He looked at her like she'd just said she wasn't human. "Well,

Miss Carly, that simply won't do." He pushed against the table and stood. Carly noticed the weakness in his core, the difference in length between his left leg and his right. Even with his injuries, he radiated power and confidence as he reached the door and opened it.

Reese paused on the threshold. "Well? Come on. You can't leave Three Rivers without seeing at least one horse."

———————

Reese had no idea why he'd invited Carly Watters to stay and see the horses. Even more surprising was that she'd agreed. He'd watched her war with something within, but in the end, she'd said yes.

*Why'd you ask her at all?* he wondered for the fifth time as he stepped onto the dirt road that led to the horse barn. He didn't know. But he did like her bright, blue eyes, her platinum hair, her purple car.

"So tell me about you," he said. "I'm sure that file gives you all my details."

"Six older brothers," Carly said. "From Amarillo. Served two deployments." Her voice caught on the last word, and Reese slid her a glance. She seemed mortified by what she'd said.

"I know I served in the Army," he said. "I know I got hurt. It's okay to talk about."

"Is it?" She peered at him like she wasn't really sure.

"Yeah, sure." Lex had assured him that her replacement was amazing. That she'd take good care of him. Reese didn't need a lot now that he'd gotten the job at Courage Reins, now that he'd signed up for free shipping and online grocery shopping. But he missed Lex. She'd always been good company for him. He wondered if his file said that.

*Lonely. A sad, lonely veteran whose best friends have four legs and long manes. Or are already married.*

"How long have you been a care coordinator?" he asked, glad when his voice didn't betray the storm of emotions stirring inside.

She gave a nervous giggle. "This is my first appointment." She froze on the gravel, and he thought she'd hurt herself in those bright heels. "I'm totally doing it wrong, aren't I?"

Reese retraced his steps back to her and hooked her elbow in his. "'Course not, Miss Carly. You're keeping me company, and that's exactly what I need right now."

She gazed up at him, and Reese's mind went into a tailspin. His pulse followed suit, and he forced himself to look away so he wouldn't say or do something stupid. He took a slow step toward the barn, relieved when Carly came with him.

He hadn't dated since he'd come home broken, three years ago. Hadn't even thought about it. Had told Chelsea no over and over when she suggested women he could take out. But now, with Carly's cold fingers pressing into his forearm, he thought maybe he was ready to take a step toward getting to know her.

"So, you?" he asked. "I do have six brothers, and they're all married and successful. Does my file say that? That I'm seventh best? The seventh sergeant in the family?"

She shook her head, her loose curls brushing his arm. Fireworks tumbled up his arm and sparked in his shoulder. He hadn't felt like this about anyone for so, so long. He hardly trusted himself to know what it meant.

"No, your file lists your family stats, but nothing about them. Where are they?"

Reese took a deep breath as they stepped out of the weak sunshine and into the barn. Just the presence of animals settled him. "You're not getting out of telling me about yourself." He led her past the first stall, heading for Elvis. He clucked his tongue at the black-and-white paint stallion.

"Oh, he's gorgeous," Carly breathed as the horse lumbered toward them.

Reese let Elvis snuffle against his hand. "He's a thoroughbred.

Won a few races before he hurt his leg." He spoke with love and reverence about the horse. "I rescued him from death. When a racehorse can't race...." He let the sentence hang there, grateful the gentle animal hadn't lost his life.

He'd been saved, the same way Reese had. Though he'd struggled to find worth inside himself, he saw it in Elvis, and he knew God had rescued them both. It had taken Reese many long months to get to that place, and a sense of gratitude filled him every time he thought about his journey.

Elvis eyed Carly, and she shrank behind Reese. "Oh, come on, Miss Carly. He won't bite."

"He's taller than I thought."

Reese turned around. "Let's go see Tabasco. He's smaller."

She went with him, sure and strong on such skinny heels. "Who names the horses?"

"Whoever owns them as foals. We don't get a lot of those here on the ranch. Our horses are retired from working or whatever. We use them for therapy." Further down the line, Tabasco waited with his head already over the fence.

"See? He's much shorter."

Carly reached hesitantly toward him, and Reese willed the bay to behave. He did, his eyes falling halfway closed as Carly stroked his cheek.

"He likes you."

Carly beamed under the compliment, and Reese wanted to make her feel like that again. "So, your family?"

"I have three sisters. Two older, and one twin, who I'm four minutes older than."

"A twin, huh?"

"Mirror twins," she said. "My hair parts on the left, hers on the right. I have a dimple on my left cheek, hers is on the right."

Reese had no idea what mirror twins meant, but before he could ask more, she said, "Basically everything Cassie does is right, while everything I do isn't."

He heard every syllable of resentment, of frustration, of sadness in her statement. In her next breath, she put on a happy smile and started asking him about the different kinds of horses.

Reese obliged and kept the conversation light and flowing. But he couldn't shake the feeling that maybe Carly Watters was as lonely as he was.

## 2

C arly pressed her lips together, regretting it when the waxy texture of her lipstick made them stick together. But she wasn't going to give Reese another detail about her life. He didn't need to know her father had also served in the Army and had been sent home in a flag-draped casket when she was only twelve years old.

That event had begun the first of many years of frustration for Carly. Her mom suddenly had to find a way to make everything work, and that meant getting a job. All the girls had lost their dad, but also now had to help in ways they hadn't previously. From age twelve until she left home, all Carly did was babysit to help keep the electricity on.

"You have time to stop by the grocery store and pick up some ice cream?" Reese's soft yet strong voice brought her out of her past.

She glanced at him, and found an unassuming look on his face as he stroked Tabasco. "I thought you said you did all your grocery shopping online."

"I do." He shrugged. "But they have a minimum order of thirty dollars, and all I need is the ice cream." He flicked a quick look at her, barely long enough to make eye contact. Something hot flared in Carly's chest. Something that spoke of attraction, but also gratitude. Reese had heard the disquiet in her statement about Cassie—Carly couldn't believe she'd even said it—and was trying to make her feel better.

"Sure, I can stop by the store for ice cream." She shifted her weight in her pinpoint heels. "What kind?"

Reese leaned against the fence as if he was suddenly too tired to stand. "What's your favorite kind? Surprise me with that."

"Do you like—?"

"Surprise me," he said, speaking over her.

A smile played with her lips, but she didn't let it win. "Okay. A surprise it is. Anything else you need?"

He stared openly at her now, and Carly couldn't decipher the emotions edging his dark chocolate-colored eyes. "What do *you* need, Miss Carly?"

The question caught her completely off-guard. No one asked her what she wanted, what she needed. She lived alone in a one-bedroom apartment in Amarillo, and she went to work everyday in a crowded, barely air conditioned office. This job was a huge promotion, one that would allow her to be freer with her debit card and help her pay off her student loans faster. One with more responsibility and greater status, even if Reese was her first—and only—client.

*For now*, she told herself. Lex had handled a half dozen veterans, but each new care coordinator only worked with one for the first couple of months. Carly didn't know what she'd do all day if Reese only needed her to pick up ice cream.

"You okay?" Reese touched her arm, shooting a current into her shoulder.

Carly jerked as if electrocuted and stumbled in her shoes. Reese latched onto her to steady her, and Carly had the strangest urge to lean into his embrace, steal his strength, absorb his warmth, breathe in the manly smell of him.

"I'm okay," she confirmed, and he dropped his hand. She focused her attention on the horse—anything to distract herself from the cowboy next to her. "Do you ride him?"

"Tabasco? Nah." Reese shook his head and stroked the horse's nose. "He's for kids. But you could ride 'im if you wanted."

Carly backed up a step as terror bolted through her. "Do I look like a little girl?"

Reese's careful appraisal of her, the way his eyes skated from her toes to her forehead, did little to cool the fire burning in Carly's core.

"Certainly not," he finally said. He cleared his throat and took a couple of steps away. "Well, come on then. If you don't want to ride Tabasco, maybe you shouldn't give him the idea that he'll get to be ridden. Hurts his feelings."

Carly cast one last look at the horse standing mutely before her. It hurt his feelings not to be ridden? Ridiculous. She followed Reese out of the barn, surprised at how quickly the man could move with his limp.

She handed him her phone without the possibility of their hands touching and watched as he put in his number and home address. He grinned at her when he texted her his garage code so she could get in the house and put the ice cream in the freezer. Then he excused himself and went into the building that housed the offices of Courage Reins.

Carly moved on numb legs back to her car, where she turned up the heat to full blast. Spring needed to arrive, or she needed to start wearing a jacket. *And a pair of boots*, she thought as she put the car in reverse.

Halfway back to town, she reached for the radio. "Stop thinking about him!" she commanded herself. She couldn't get Sergeant Reese Sanders out of her head, and the idea annoyed her. She wasn't looking for another cowboy to stomp all over her heart with his weathered cowboy boots, spurs and all. She'd done that once, thank you very much.

Tanner's face filled her mind, only fueling Carly's frustration. She'd rather forget their two-year relationship that had ended when he joined the professional rodeo circuit and broken up with her through a text.

Two years, and all she got was a text. Cowboys definitely weren't Carly's type.

She managed to banish the thoughts of Tanner, but as she pulled into the parking lot of the only grocery store in Three Rivers, Reese snuck back into her mind. She stood in front of the freezers for what seemed like an hour, trying to decide which flavor of ice cream the man would enjoy.

Thinking through his file, she couldn't recall a single fact that would lead her to the right choice. Chocolate? Strawberry? Something with candy?

In the end, she selected lime sherbet—her favorite—and a carton of peanut butter cup ice cream, complete with fudge ribbons. As she checked out, she hoped he didn't have a nut allergy. She almost went back, but determined not to. He should've said something if he couldn't have nuts.

With his address programmed into her GPS, she drove to his house. In his driveway, she texted, *You don't have a nut allergy, right?* and waited for him to respond.

*Nope.*

Finally able to relax, she punched in the garage code and entered the sergeant's house. She wasn't sure what to expect, but a crisp, sterile scent in the air wasn't it. The kitchen counter waited without a single item on it. No dirty dishes sat in the sink. The living room held a couch and two armchairs, one of which had folded blankets on it. She couldn't even find a speck of dust.

She opened the fridge and found every item arranged just so, almost like Reese had chalk lines the containers fit into. The freezer held little, leaving lots of room for the two cartons of sweets she'd bought. She put the ice cream away and laid the receipt on the counter. She stood in his space and took a deep breath. The peace and familiarity she felt here should've surprised her. Instead, all it did was remind her of what she didn't have.

She spun on her toe and left his house. She hated small towns and loathed cowboys, and just because Reese reminded her of her father—down to his dark hair and obsession with neatness—couldn't convince her to leave the life she'd been building for the past eight years.

---

REESE SAT BEHIND THE DESK AT COURAGE REINS, A PENCIL IN HIS hand as he sketched, but his mind tumbling through scenarios that featured Carly Watters. He could call her and ask her to help him with his yard work. Text her and say he needed to go to Amarillo and buy some new boots. Ask her to come back out to the ranch for one of his riding sessions.

He did nothing but keep his pencil moving over the paper. Soon enough, Tabasco came to life, with a beautiful woman standing in front of him, a look of apprehension and wonder on her face.

"Reese." Pete's voice shattered the illusions in Reese's mind. He fisted the art before his boss could see it.

"Yeah?" He glanced up at the same time he commanded himself not to be embarrassed. So he liked Carly Watters. What man wouldn't? Tall and curvy and blonde. Reese licked his lips. "What's up?"

"Stephen's coming in a half hour."

"Stephen, right." Reese stood and moved to the cabinet built into the wall behind him. The patient files filled most of the space now, and Reese thumbed through the N's for Stephen Newman.

"I want you to work with him." Pete knocked on the counter a couple of times. "You up for that?"

Reese straightened as much as his injury would allow him to. "You want me to work with him?"

"Yeah," Pete said. "Lawrence will be there to assist, but I think you're ready to start working with patients. Especially other veterans." His steady gaze, the confidence in his voice, didn't escape Reese's attention. Pete believed in him. He always had, right back to the very first time Reese had come out to Three Rivers and Courage Reins for his first riding appointment.

"Okay." Reese gripped Stephen's file.

"Okay." Pete grinned and tapped his cowboy hat. "Read through the notes on his last session, and I think you'll be good to go." He continued around the counter toward the hall that led to the indoor training facility. "Oh, and he needs to meet with Doctor Parchman next time he's out. So be sure to schedule that before he leaves."

"You got it," Reese said, and Pete ducked through the door.

Reese sat down and opened Stephen's file. Before he started reading, he bowed his head and offered a prayer of thanks. Thanks for this life he had now. Thanks for his health. Thanks for his body, his mind. Thanks that he'd been able to find a place where he could be himself in this world.

Emotion choked his throat and his thoughts, and Reese opened his eyes and started reading the notes from Stephen's last session.

Twenty minutes later, he leaned in the barn's entrance, waiting. Pete had a policy to always be ready when the patients arrived, and Reese wasn't going to mess it up on his first time. Lawrence puttered around with the horses behind him, but Stephen would be saddling his horse himself after he arrived.

Reese appreciated always having someone there to welcome him, and he thought of Pete's wife, Chelsea. She'd made him feel comfortable and accepted at Three Rivers, long before he felt that way inside his own skin. She'd often greeted him while Pete readied the horses, and Reese felt involved in something bigger than himself. He needed that, needed to be beyond his own selfish sphere, and he made a mental note to thank Pete for allowing him to work with the patients.

That wasn't technically part of his job description, but Pete seemed to know what Reese needed without having to ask.

A car came down the lane, but it wasn't Stephen's truck. Reese recognized the vehicle even before it made the turn toward the homestead. Squire and Kelly Ackerman had arrived. A smile graced Reese's face. He didn't know Major Ackerman as well as some of the other men at Courage Reins or on the ranch, but he knew enough to respect the man.

Pete exited Courage Reins and waved to Reese as he headed toward the homestead. A few cowhands followed him and a large moving truck ambled into the driveway. Squire had finished his veterinary degree and was finally moving back to Three Rivers.

Garth Ahlstrom, the foreman of the ranch, paused near Reese. "How's it going, Reese?" he asked.

"Good," he said. "Squire's back."

Garth grinned. "Yeah. 'Bout time. I've been waitin' on him for years."

"I didn't realize they were moving in today." Reese squinted into the sunlight, wondering if he'd been left out on purpose because he couldn't help unpack much. He stuffed the resentful thoughts away. The people in Three Rivers didn't treat him as broken.

"No one did," Garth said. "Apparently Squire texted Pete ten minutes ago and said they were pullin' in." Garth clapped his hand on Reese's shoulder. "Wish I would'a known. I've got most of my boys out in the branding fields."

"Maybe Squire didn't want everyone on the ranch makin' a big deal out it."

Garth chuckled. "I'm sure that's true. But with Kelly pregnant, they'll need the help."

"Send Finn over to help with the horses," Reese said.

"Stephen's coming, and he has a son the same age, so he won't mind."

Garth nodded his approval and headed toward the homestead. He'd just entered the kitchen when Stephen pulled into the Courage Reins parking lot. Reese took a tentative step on his shorter leg, giving it a moment to adjust to the movement.

"Stephen," he said. "I'm gonna work with you today."

Stephen, a tall, dark-skinned man unfolded himself from the car. "Great," he said with his booming voice. A commanding officer, Stephen had lost his left leg in a building collapse. He wore a prosthetic and walked with a limp slightly less severe than Reese's.

"How are things?" Reese asked as they hobbled into the barn.

"Good enough," Stephen said. "Lost Lex." His voice quieted on the last two words. "I'm gonna miss that woman."

"She was the best," Reese agreed. "But she had a great opportunity to work in Denver. Who'd you get for your new care coordinator?"

"Haven't heard yet. You?"

"Yeah, I met with a woman named Carly Watters today." He made his voice as nonchalant as possible. "Seemed...nice."

"So she's new." Stephen chuckled. "I'm sure I'll get someone new too. Lex said they've had a lot of turnover in their office the past few months."

Reese had been told that too. "Carly seemed to know what she was doing." He stopped in front of Hank's stall. "You're saddling and everything today, Commander."

Stephen clucked at Hank and held out his hand. The bay stallion with a black mane and tail snuffled at Stephen's fingers, searching for any hint of sugar. "I'll give you a treat after," Stephen said in a voice usually reserved for babies. "Come on, now." He unlatched the gate and entered the stall with Hank. He had him saddled and ready in only a few minutes, and though Reese hadn't taught him any of it, pride swelled in his chest.

He knew what it was like to come home broken, to feel like nobody cared, like nothing mattered. Stephen had a wife and two kids, but he still suffered through the same depression and mental issues as Reese had.

Doing something—even something as mundane as saddling a horse, or riding a horse—brought a sense of accomplishment that helped more than words could say.

"Let's ride," Reese said as he reached for Peony's reins. Lawrence had her ready, and he disappeared down the hall leading to the outdoor arena. Reese let Stephen take Hank out first, then he led Peony into the arena. He had to use the fence to mount up, but he'd done it so often, it only took seconds now.

"Lawrence says you're ready to trot," Reese called to Stephen. The man turned toward him with surprise in his eyes.

"I am?"

Reese smiled, infusing a dose of Chelsea's charm into the gesture. She'd always believed in him too. "I think you are, Commander."

"All right." Stephen set his mouth in a determined line. "Let's do it."

Reese taught him how to hold his reins with a looser grip, how to use the stirrups to lift himself the slightest bit. Lawrence stepped in and reminded them both to keep the lines loose so as to not jam up the horses. Reese nodded, and he moved Peony into a trot first to demonstrate.

He stopped her at the end of the arena, the scent of spring in the air intoxicating. Reese needed to get outside the office walls more often. "Okay, Stephen. Your turn."

Stephen managed to get Hank into a trot fairly easily, but the horse quickly dropped back to a walk. Reese frowned. Hank was a runner—he'd seen Chelsea ride him as he streaked around the arena, his black mane flying behind him like ribbons.

"Try again," he said.

Again, Stephen got the horse to a trot, and this time, Hank

went around the arena once before slowing again. Reese moved Peony into the ring, intending to check Hank. Perhaps he should put Stephen on another horse; maybe Hank wasn't feeling well today.

Reese increased Peony to a trot, his mind racing through possibilities, when he realized Stephen had turned Hank and urged him to a trot too.

A cry of terror rent the air, and Hank reared back. Reese realized the scream had come from Hank's throat at the same time he watched Stephen slip from the saddle.

Lawrence shouted; Hank shot forward; Reese blinked, blinked. In less than a heartbeat, he knew he was in trouble. He tried to swing Peony out of Hank's way, but he was too late. Hank bore down on them, swerving away at the last minute. Unfortunately, the normally calm and peaceful Peony swung in the same direction.

Hank knocked into her, sending her off-balance. Reese knew he was going to fall before it happened. He gripped the reins tighter—his first mistake.

Another inhuman shriek tore through his ears as he landed on the packed earth of the arena, Peony on top of him. Something tore in his abdomen; pain screamed up to the top of his head and down to the heels of his feet.

He blinked into the blue sky, but couldn't seem to focus on anything. He heard the pounding of boots. Lawrence's tan face appeared in his vision, his mouth moving in the shape of *Reese? You okay, Reese?*

But Reese wasn't okay. He couldn't move. Peony scrambled on top of him, planting one hoof directly on his breastbone and finally pushing herself up and away. His chest caved; his lungs sputtered; his eyes drifted closed.

The scent of burning hair and melted metal filled his nose. Diesel fuel dripped onto his hair. The screams of dying men filled his ears. Fire licked his skin, cascaded through his muscles, consumed his hip. But he couldn't get out of the tank.

Couldn't move.

Couldn't see.

Couldn't breathe.

## 3

Carly settled behind the desk in her cubicle and set to work fixing Reese's file. Once she finished, she opened the first of three new folders that had been stacked on her desk while she'd been out at Three Rivers. She scanned the first page, realizing that she'd been assigned another veteran.

*Three* more veterans. She smiled to herself as she lost herself in their histories, their service, their current needs. As she did, she realized all three of them went out to Courage Reins for equine therapy. Her heart sank a notch as she searched for their addresses. Her spirits lifted again when she realized they lived here in Amarillo, same as her. Relief that she wouldn't have to drive out to Three Rivers every day spread through her. And these veterans weren't cowboys either. They were simply taking advantage of the veteran services Courage Reins offered.

Her phone rang as she finished the last file. An unknown number—which Carly usually sent to voice mail—but she thumbed the line open anyway. "Carly Watters," she said.

"Hello," a male voice said, carrying an undercurrent of emotion Carly couldn't quite identify. "Are you Reese Sanders' veteran care coordinator?"

Carly sat up straighter. "Yes."

"I need the numbers for his family," the man said. "They're not in his phone, and well...he's been hurt."

"Hurt?" Carly's voice strayed into an upper octave. She reached for her purse and fumbled for her keys. "Hurt how?"

"He fell off a horse."

"Can I speak to him?"

"No, ma'am. He's unconscious, on the way to the hospital in Three Rivers. I need to call his family and let them know. But like I said, he doesn't have their numbers in his phone. My wife suggested I call his care coordinator, and well, he had your number in his phone."

A pinpoint of warmth penetrated the icy feeling spreading through Carly's chest. "Who is this?" she asked as she threw the new files, along with Reese's, into her purse. "I can give you the number, but I should know who I'm giving it to." At least she thought she could give out the phone number. She stood and looked for her supervisor. She caught Lindsay's eye and beckoned her over, then grabbed her laptop charger and added that to her bag.

"Peter Marshall, ma'am. I'm Reese's boss, and friend. He was my first patient at Courage Reins." Carly identified the emotion in Peter's voice—worry, concern, fear.

"One moment," she said. She hurried to explain the situation to Lindsay, who authorized her to give out the number.

"And then get to Three Rivers," Lindsay said. "Reese doesn't have much contact with his family, and he'll need help."

Carly nodded, her heart playing a game of teeter totter in her chest. It flung itself to the back of her throat at the thought of seeing Reese again so soon, but dropped to the bottom of her gut at having to return to the Podunk town where he lived.

She swiped her laptop into the crook of her arm and headed for the door as she recited the contact number of Reese's family to Peter Marshall. Five minutes later, she had the hospital's address in her GPS and had once again set her car on the two-lane highway that took her west of the city she loved.

---

Upon arriving at the hospital, it wasn't hard to find those waiting to hear about Reese. Every man in the small group clustered in the corner wore a cowboy hat, cowboy boots, and flannel in an assortment of colors.

"Excuse me?" She tugged at the hem of her blouse as they turned toward her. "I'm Carly Watters, Sergeant Sanders' veteran care coordinator." She glanced over her shoulder. "Are you waiting on him?"

A muscled man stood. "I'm Pete Marshall," he said, extending his hand for her to shake. She noticed the puckered scars marring his skin. "They took him back a while ago. We haven't heard anything."

"Did you get in touch with his family?" Carly took the seat Pete gestured her toward.

"I did, thank you, Miss Carly. They're on their way as well. Should be here soon." He took off his hat and raked his hands over his mostly shaved blond hair. "They're out of Amarillo, too. Didn't you come that far?"

"Yes, sir," she said. "But I may have driven a bit over the speed limit." She tossed him a tight smile, wondering what had compelled her to get here so quickly. "What happened?"

"I'm not all the way sure," Pete said. "I wasn't there. But he was working with another patient, and they both got thrown."

Carly sucked in a breath. "Is the other patient okay?"

"He's here too," Pete said. "But he never lost consciousness. He doesn't have the same war injuries Reese does. Lost his leg is all."

*Lost his leg is all.* The words, though spoken with reverence and kindness, felt too flippant. Carly's mind stumbled with the information.

"It wasn't Stephen Newman, was it?"

Pete looked at her, surprise in his eyes. "Yeah. How did you know?"

She lifted Reese's folder. "I just read his file this afternoon. I just got assigned to be his care coordinator too."

"Convenient," Pete said.

"Yeah," Carly agreed. She settled back in her chair, a swarm of ants swimming in her stomach.

A few minutes later, a woman and two children entered the waiting area. Carly recognized them from Stephen's file, but Pete stood and crossed the room to greet them. When he turned back to lead them over to the group, tears glistened in his eyes.

"He owns Courage Reins," the cowboy next to her whispered. "Feels responsible."

Pieces clicked together as Pete gestured to her. "This is Stephen's veteran care coordinator," he said. "Miss Carly...uh...."

"Watters." Carly stood. "I just got Stephen's case this afternoon. I'm here for whatever he needs."

The woman nodded and swiped at her eyes as tears threatened to escape. Carly felt completely out of her league. How could she possibly help this family?

A dark-haired woman came through the door, and Pete stepped away to intercept her. Carly watched their exchange; the concern in the woman's eyes, the deep breath Pete took as if he hadn't been breathing before, the loving way they embraced.

He brought her toward the group. "Carly, this is my wife, Chelsea."

Carly noticed the barely-there baby bump and the red-rimmed eyes Chelsea bore. "Nice to meet you. You must know Reese and Stephen."

Chelsea swallowed and nodded. "Reese was our first patient." She tilted her head back to look at Pete. "He has to be okay."

"He'll be okay," Pete murmured, his mouth only inches from his wife's. A surge of jealousy coated Carly's tongue. She tried to swallow it away, but it proved too difficult. She'd imagined herself in this exact situation too many times over the course of her two-year relationship with Tanner.

She let her gaze linger on Chelsea's baby bump for another few seconds before finding a seat further down the row. Minutes ticked by. The cowboys made a somber lot, with no discussion or chit-chat. Even Pete answered Chelsea's whispered questions with one-word answers.

Finally, after an hour of waiting, a man wearing blue scrubs came through the door. He held a clipboard in his hand and called, "Reese Sanders?"

Carly didn't tell her body to stand, but she did. Pete did too. As did Chelsea, all the Newman family, and every cowboy in the waiting room. Carly looked at them, really looked, and saw their love and concern for Reese.

The doctor moved toward them. "Well, you can't all come back." He smiled. "But he's out of danger and awake. Who wants the official report?"

Pete's hand went up. "We can all hear, Doctor. How is he?"

"Any family here?" The doctor scanned the small crowd.

Carly's fingers worried over themselves. His family should've been able to make it by now. She hadn't driven that fast.

"Not yet," Pete said.

The doctor frowned. "Well, he said I could tell anyone wearing a cowboy hat the news, so I guess you lot will do." He gave them another smile. "Truth is, we're not sure of the extent of the damage, especially in his back. He can move right now, but when he was brought in, I thought he was paralyzed."

Carly's head spun. Paralyzed.

*No.*

"He's got three broken ribs from where the horse stepped on him, and that'll cause him quite a bit of pain. He's bruised. He's lost some elasticity in his abdomenal wall. He's...." The doctor looked down at his clipboard and cleared his throat. "His ribs will heal. His bruises will fade. He'll be able to get his range of motion back, especially through the equine therapy. But he's understandably upset."

Pete and Chelsea exchanged a nervous glance, and Chelsea's tears made an appearance. Carly felt closed off from the situation. A bystander. An outsider. For some reason, she wanted that to change. She wanted to help Reese recover, regain the life he'd had at Courage Reins.

"I'm prescribing an anti-depressant, but I'm not sure he'll take it. Reese is a bit...."

"Stubborn?" Pete supplied.

"I'll make sure he takes it." Two heartbeats passed before Carly realized *she'd* spoken the words. But no one contradicted her.

"I'm keeping him overnight so I can check on his condition in the morning," the doctor continued. "If he can still move his legs and feel the pricks in his feet, he'll be free to go."

"Is there a possibility he could be paralyzed?" Chelsea asked. "I mean, now? It could happen even though he's stable now?"

"Yes," the doctor said. "He hurt his hip and back in Kandahar. The nerves there have moved and relocated. Some are in his vertebrae where they shouldn't be. As he continues to heal, they could shift again. He could be fine one day, and unable to move the next." He wore a look of genuine empathy, and his smooth voice could've soothed wounds. "We'll watch him tomorrow, and he'll need to come back in every few days for a while."

"I can do that too," Carly said, with a glance toward Stephen's family. "What about Commander Newman? How is he?"

His wife stepped forward, and slipped her fingers into Carly's. Her grip could've cracked an egg, but Carly didn't complain.

The doctor sent a faint smile in her direction. "Mister Newman is cleared to go home. He's got bruises on his legs and back, but he'll heal fine. No signs of a concussion. No broken bones. No internal back pain—only surface level injuries." The doors behind him pushed open. "Ah, here he is."

His wife and kids hurried toward him, and Carly stayed put so they could have their reunion with some privacy. She watched them with a melting heart, glad beyond description that one of her veterans wasn't further injured.

Pete stepped next to her, too close to be casual. "You're going to help Reese with his pills? Getting to his doctor's appointments? All of it?" His whispered growl barely met her ears.

She didn't turn toward him. "Yes, sir."

"You live here?"

Carly's heart beat out an erratic pulse. She stepped back and looked up at the man. He was big, and strong, and imposing, yet she felt that underneath all that lived and beat a heart that cared a lot about Reese.

"Not yet," she said. "But it feels like a good time to move."

Pete didn't get a chance to respond. The doctor said he could take a few people back to see Reese, and Carly stepped toward him. "I want to go."

"Me too," Chelsea said.

"And you, Lieutenant Marshall?"

Pete—a lieutenant—nodded. He gestured Carly to go in front of him, his bright green eyes sizing her up and making a judgment. She hoped it was a good one, but if it wasn't, she'd work hard to prove him wrong.

She could help Reese. She would, even if it meant moving to small-town Three Rivers.

---

REESE WASN'T SURPRISED TO SEE CHELSEA PEER AROUND THE corner of the curtain. His face broke into the best grin he could manage at the sight of her. She'd always soothed him, from the moment he met her that first time at Courage Reins.

"Chelsea," he said. "Come on over. I'm okay."

She wiped her tears as she moved toward him. "It's just my hormones." She half-laughed, half-sobbed. "I know you're okay." She bent down and placed a tender kiss to his forehead. "But I also know you're really not."

Thankfully, she kept her voice low with her last words, because a blonde woman had appeared in his peripheral vision. "Carly?"

Chelsea stepped back to make room for the other woman.

"Lieutenant Marshall called me," she said, stopping a healthy distance away and appraising his prone form. "I bet you need more than ice cream now, don't you, Sergeant?" A genuine smile accompanied her question, and Reese felt lighter with her flirtatious words.

"They won't let me eat," he said, drawing his eyebrows into a frown. "So I hope you got me something good."

"It's a surprise," she said as Pete came around the corner. The life whooshed out of him at the sight of the lieutenant, the anguished look on his face, the wetness in the corners of his eyes.

"Reese."

"It's not your fault, Pete," Reese said. "It's not mine, either. I still don't quite know what happened. How's Stephen?" He managed to get all the words out without a tremor in his voice, and by the time he stopped speaking he'd schooled his emotions.

Carly stepped back and faded into the background as Pete joined Chelsea at Reese's side.

"I feel like it's my fault. I asked you to work with Stephen."

Chelsea threaded her fingers through Pete's, and a stab of jealousy bolted through Reese. He thought about holding Carly's hand, and what it might feel like since it had been so long since he'd done anything remotely close to holding hands with a woman. Heat crept into his face when he realized Pete had cocked an eyebrow at him.

"What?" Reese asked.

Pete glanced at Carly over his shoulder. "I asked if you needed anything. I can smuggle in a hamburger. I'm not afraid." His mouth quirked up in a half-smile.

The thought of eating anything more than the broth and gelatin the nurses had promised to bring him as soon as he could get a permanent room made his stomach twist. "I'm good."

Carly stepped forward. "That's what he says when he needs something."

A flash of annoyance covered his previous desire to hold her hand. "I'm fine."

"Fine is worse than good." Chelsea cocked her hip and studied him. He didn't like it. Didn't like the three of them in here, assessing him, trying to figure out what they could bring to make him better. There wasn't anything any of them could do, unless they could turn back time and stop him from stalling next to that fateful building to catch his breath and check his surroundings. He'd had zero warning of the explosion that left his hip shattered and his confidence in jagged pieces.

"We'll go," Pete said. He ushered Chelsea toward the edge of the curtain, only pausing to turn back and say, "We'll be back tomorrow to help you get home."

"Oh, I can do that," Carly said. "I'll be staying in town tonight, so I can make sure Sergeant Sanders has everything he needs."

Reese simultaneously wanted Carly to be the one to help him get home, while at the same time, he never wanted her to witness his weaknesses. He looked away without confirming anything.

"Okay," Pete said, leaving Reese alone with Carly. A muscle in his jaw jumped, ached as he bit down hard.

"You don't have—" he started at the same time she asked, "Why didn't your parents come?"

Was she trying to make him feel worse? It hadn't escaped his attention that his only visitors weren't blood related. He shrugged and lay back against his pillows, forcing a fake yawn through his lips.

"I'll find out what time to come tomorrow," Carly said, taking the hint. "See you in the morning, Sergeant Sanders."

"You don't have to come tomorrow," he said, finally looking in her direction again.

Her lips flattened into a pretty pink line, and her bright blue eyes blazed with a defiant fire. Reese's pulse kicked up a notch, a fact the machine at his bedside testified of.

Carly didn't glance at it. "I'll be here, Sergeant, no matter what you say." She spun in her purple heels and marched past the curtain, finally leaving Reese to his own thoughts.

An hour later, a nurse named Summer woke him with the words, "Reese, your father is here. We just got you a room, so we're going to move you up there and he'll meet us there."

A sense of relief painted his insides. His dad had come. Reese had known he would, but he hadn't expected him until morning. His mom's anxiety when it came to Reese was nearly debilitating —one of the many reasons Reese had moved to Three Rivers over three years ago.

"Did my mom come?"

"Just your dad." Summer smiled at him and nodded to another man in scrubs. "Jeremy, you get the bed, and I'll wheel this equipment with us."

Reese kept his eyes closed on the journey toward his room, letting Summer shoulder the conversation. She told him what floor he'd be on, and who his night nurse would be, and when he could have more pain meds.

He wanted another dose right now. And more in an hour. Anything to keep his mind numb and his muscles free from pain. He dismissed the thoughts quickly, recognizing the dark rabbit hole his mind could become if he allowed such desires to remain.

As Summer quieted and his bed rolled to a stop, Reese sent a prayer heavenward. *Help me, Lord.* With his mind in such a dark place, he couldn't think much more than that.

Summer and Jeremy left, and his dad entered not two seconds later. "Reese." He joined him at his side, and swiped the hair off Reese's forehead. Reese leaned into his father's touch, finally allowing a single tear to escape the corner of his eye.

"Dad."

"I'm sorry it took me so long to come. Mom...had a hard time."

Reese nodded, the trench of despair he'd been holding back rising, rising, rising, ready to be released. With his dad, Reese didn't have to hide his emotions. With his dad, he knew he was safe to weep, safe to say he was afraid, safe to be weak and lonely and broken.

"The doctor says there's a chance of paralysis." His dad pulled a chair closer. "How do you feel?"

"I'm okay," Reese said, his voice nasal as the tears continued to leak down his cheeks. "I can feel my legs and move them and everything. When I first woke up, I couldn't. After a few minutes, they started to tingle and then I could feel them fine."

"He's worried about it."

"I know." Reese turned his head away when a nurse entered. His dad stood and moved to the end of the bed, shielding him from the woman.

"I'm Jacinda," she said. "I'll be your nurse for the evening. How's your pain, Mister Sanders?"

"Fine," Reese said, his voice still somewhat thick.

"They've got a tray of food in the hall for you. Is now a good time?"

"Yes."

She wheeled it in, made a note on the whiteboard on the wall, and left him and his dad alone again. His dad positioned the tray on the wheeled table and moved it in front of Reese. "Looks like chicken broth, orange gelatin, and...." He picked up a small plastic cup with a tin foil lid. "Frozen fruit sorbet." He flashed a quick, Army smile. "Sounds delicious."

"Can you get me some water?" He lifted the water bottle the hospital would probably charge him twenty dollars for, and his dad took it.

"Sure thing, son. Be right back."

Being alone, and awake, was torture. Reese reached for the remote and turned on the TV mounted to the wall above the door, but it was poor company. He switched it off when his father returned.

"They have the good pebble ice here." He set the water bottle on the table and took up his position in the armchair next to the bed.

"You stayin' the night?" Reese asked, not bothering to keep the hope from entering his tone.

"Of course." His dad reached over and put his hand on Reese's forearm. "You'll recover, Reese. I know it seems like you won't right now, but you will."

Reese nodded, those awful tears burning his eyes again. He drank his broth and ate his gelatin and scooped out the fruit sorbet while his father told stories of his time in the first Iraq war. He hadn't come home with physical injuries, but Reese knew war inflicted more wounds than eyes could see.

He closed his eyes as his dad began a new tale about Ian, Reese's oldest brother who lived in Cheyenne. With Carly's cute curls and pretty face floating through his mind and his dad's soothing voice in his ear, he fell into a dreamless sleep.

## 4

Carly settled at the small table in her hotel room and set up her office. Laptop, plugged in and with an Internet browser open. Phone, charged and with the volume on high. Notebook, on a fresh page with a pen in her hand, ready to write.

She dialed Lindsay, her nerves bouncing but her confidence high. "Hey, Lindsay," she said when her boss picked up. "I'm in Three Rivers, and well, Sergeant Sanders's injuries are pretty severe."

She took a deep breath, the next thing she needed to say making her insides quake. "I'd like to stay here for a while, make sure he's settled in."

"Okay," Lindsay said.

"I just got three new veterans today, but they all come out to Courage Reins for therapy. I'm thinking I'll ask the director there —his name's Pete Marshall—if I can meet with them while they're already on-site, at the facility."

"Sounds like you've thought of everything."

Carly chuckled, the sound too high and girlish for her liking. But she couldn't help that her nerves had infused her voice.

"Well, maybe not everything. But Stephen Newman was released tonight, and he should be fine." She paused, sure Reese wouldn't bounce back as quickly as Stephen would.

"Reese Sanders will be fine too, Carly," Lindsay said. "It'll just take him longer. And it's your job to make sure he has everything he needs."

"Right," Carly said. "I visited with him for a few minutes, and I'll be there tomorrow to help him get home, and...whatever else he needs." She wasn't entirely sure what the sergeant would need, but she hoped it involved an hour or two of conversation. She enjoyed his steady strength, the warm timbre of his voice, the handsome shape of his jaw.

She cleared her throat, wishing the unprofessional thoughts could be dislodged as easily. "I probably won't be in the office for several days."

"That's fine." A clatter came through the line. "I don't have my files at home, but I believe your vets have appointments at Courage Reins this week."

Carly pulled her files closer. "They do. I'll be sure to check in with them." Though the thought of driving forty minutes out to the ranch sent her stomach into a tailspin. At least the commute had been shortened considerably by her staying in town.

*Maybe you should move here.* The thought entered her mind and stabbed its way around, causing her heart rate to spike and her fingers to fumble the phone.

"I have to go," she said. "I'll be sure to check in."

"Good luck, Carly," Lindsay said warmly before she hung up.

Carly stared at her phone, sure its cellular waves had caused her brain to malfunction. She most definitely should not move to Three Rivers. The town only had one grocery store, for crying out loud.

No, she'd stay for a few days, until Reese was resting comfortably at home, with stocked cabinets, paid bills, a trimmed lawn, and all the ice cream he could possibly eat. Then she'd skedaddle back to her real life in the city.

Sadness tugged at her conscious as Reese's drawn face filled her mind's eye. She touched two fingers right above her pulse, wondering why the thought of leaving him here brought such melancholy.

As quickly as she'd let the dark clouds descend, she pushed them away. "Better get to the store before it closes." Surely the grocer wasn't an all-night joint like the ones in Amarillo, and she didn't even have a toothbrush for her stay.

A half hour later, she hurried toward the check-out. She was the only person left in the grocery store, and the manager had announced that they'd be closing twice already. The hotel where she'd booked four nights served breakfast, but Carly couldn't afford to eat out twice a day. She loaded two boxes of granola bars, a case of protein shakes, a loaf of bread, a bottle of honey and one of peanut butter, and a bag of apples onto the belt. Her toiletries came next—deodorant, toothbrush and paste, shampoo, conditioner, and an assortment of makeup.

She'd literally left Amarillo with only her office supplies. But she could survive. She had on much less before.

"Sorry," she said to the woman ringing up her items. "I'm staying in town for a few days, totally last minute, and I don't have anything."

The woman—Harriett by her nametag—smiled as she ran the bread across the scanner. "What brings y'all to Three Rivers?"

Carly smiled at the Texan twang of the woman, though she'd be mortified if she sounded like that. "I'm a veteran care coordinator, and one of my men got hurt."

Harriett covered her heart with her palm. "Oh, bless his heart. Will he be okay?"

"With time." Carly smiled as Harriett finished and said the total. Her grin hitched at the high number, but Carly swiped her debit card like she owned a tree that grew money. She'd get reimbursed. Eventually. She just needed to float for a while.

Back in the safety of her hotel room, Carly put her food and toiletries away before collapsing on the bed. Today had been exhausting, what with all the driving from Amarillo to Three Rivers and back, the wait in the hospital, and the strong, magnetic pull that drew her ever closer to Reese Sanders.

"Get a grip," she told herself as she got up and retrieved her laptop from the table. "He's a cowboy—strike one. And your client—strike two."

As she clicked around on social media, she couldn't come up with a third strike, which left a hole of hope in her hollow heart.

---

THE NEXT MORNING, CARLY ARRIVED AT THE HOSPITAL WITH TWO cups of dark coffee—from the only drive-through coffee establishment she could find. And she'd driven to the very southern edge of town to do it.

After finding out which room Reese had been assigned, she rode the elevator up and added a bounce to her step and a smile to her face as she prepared to meet him.

She knocked on the door, which stood open about an inch. She poked her head around the door before it opened all the way, hoping Reese was awake and decent. He was.

But he was not alone. An older man with shoulders just as broad, the same beautiful jaw, the same dark-diamond eyes, sat in the only armchair in the room.

Reese just blinked at her, the breakfast tray in front of him forgotten.

"Good morning," she chirped. "I brought you coffee. Two shots of cream." She set the travel mug on his tray and stepped back as far as the wall would allow her. She looked at the older gentleman, obviously Reese's father.

She extended her hand. "I'm Carly Watters, Reese's veteran care coordinator. You must be his father." She grinned for all she was worth, mentally commanding her heartbeat to *settle down!* "Another Sergeant Sanders."

The man smiled and shook her hand. "Nice to meet you, ma'am." He glanced at his son, but Reese seemed frozen in time, his eyes fixated on Carly.

"How did you know I take cream in my coffee?" His quiet question drove a spike of desire through Carly.

She wagged her finger at him. "You gave me the code to your garage, Mister. Can't be upset if I poked around in your refrigerator." She added a laugh to the end of the statement.

He didn't join her, the way she wished he would. Instead, he picked up the coffee cup and took a long drink. He sighed after he swallowed. "Sugar, too."

She liked the way he said the word sugar. Wondered how it would sound if he called her his sugar moments before he kissed her. She blinked the fantasy away as a blush rose through her neck and into her face.

"Heard anything from the doctor yet?" she asked, her voice tight.

"Not yet." His father stepped to the side. "You should sit, Miss Watters. It is Miss Watters, isn't it? You're not married?"

"Dad," Reese muttered.

"Not married," Carly said with a smile. "And I don't need to take your chair. I just came to see what time Reese would be cleared to go. I can ask at the nurse's station." She took a step toward the door. "Anything you need me to get ready at your house?"

Reese shook his head with stiff movements. "I'm good."

"You do keep a tight ship," she said. "Maybe I can move your pillows to the living room. Make sure you have the movies you want. I don't think you'll be up and about for a few days." She waited for him to growl that he was fine, the way he had last night.

His eyes darkened as a shadow crossed through his expression. "You think I'm just going to lie around and watch TV?"

Carly glanced at his father, who watched her without emotion. "That's what I would do if I had three broken ribs."

"Son—" his dad started.

"I can take care of myself," Reese said over him. "My dad's here. I have friends. I don't need you."

His words bit, clawed, tore through her cheerful façade. She retreated to the door. "Okay. I'll just check with the nurse, and I'll see you later." She managed to slip through the door before her face crumpled, before her voice broke, before he could see how much his words had hurt her.

---

REESE EXHALED AS THE DOOR CLOSED BEHIND CARLY.

"Reese, that was downright rude," his dad said. "She's just doin' her job."

"I don't need her." Reese glared at the empty space where she'd just stood, then at the delicious coffee she'd brought him. He adored Java Joe's dark roast blend. How had she known that? Surely his refrigerator hadn't told her he liked two shots of pure cream, with one scoop of raw sugar, not granulated. So how had she known?

"You might need her," his father said. "I can't stay here forever, and you have a lot of healing to do."

"She doesn't live here either," he said. "I'll manage on my own. Like I said, I have friends." He didn't detail that all his friends lived forty minutes away, out at Three Rivers Ranch. He didn't want to add to his dad's worries any more than he already had.

"She isn't married."

"Thanks for that, by the way," Reese said. "I'm not interested." But, oh, he was. Was he that transparent? Had his dad seen something that triggered the question? Reese realized he *had* stared at Carly like she was a heavenly vision when she walked through the door. He couldn't help it. She wore the same clothes as yesterday, but she'd straightened her hair and done something darker and different with her makeup. He'd liked what he'd seen yesterday, and today's look only added to her allure.

Her constant cheerfulness grated at him, though. No one could be so happy all the time. He'd seen flashes of her discontent, and it drove him to want to know more about her. About her past, about her twin, *everything* about her.

The doctor entered the room, with two nurses behind him. "I'm Doctor Kingsman. How're the legs this morning, Reese?"

"Good," he said. "No tingles. No problems." Maybe if he spoke in short sentences, he could get out of here.

"Did he get up and walk around last night?" Doctor Kingsman aimed his question at the nurses.

"No. His ribs needed more time. He probably can now, though." Jacinda spoke in a placating tone, the same as she had the couple of times she'd come in to check on him throughout the night.

"Let's give it a try." The doctor moved to Reese's bedside while a nurse exited the room. Jacinda flipped on all the lights and wrote something in his chart.

"Legs over the side," Doctor Kingsman said. "Tawny's gone to get the IV stand."

Reese complied, the movement sending a wisp of fire through his hip, back, and chest. He sucked in a breath and held it before forcing it out. A single toe on his right foot felt numb, tingly. He ignored it, and clamped his mouth shut.

Tawny returned a few moments later, and she transferred his IV line to a tall, metal stand that had a twelve-inch pole sticking out horizontally.

Reese put his right hand on the pole and touched his feet to the cold floor. He carefully put his weight on his legs, same as he'd done in Germany after the bombing. He seized onto the thought. He'd done this before. This exact thing—but worse.

His left hand reached out, and his dad took it. Gratitude filled Reese. He could recover from this setback. He hadn't had help in Germany, only letters and emails and Facetime conversations. With his dad here, and his friends at Courage Reins, he would be back at work and back riding Peony in no time.

A slice of discomfort shot through his back as he used his father's strength to stand. A groan tore through his throat.

"Go slow, son," his dad murmured.

"You okay?" Doctor Kingsman asked. "When's the last time he had pain meds?"

"Three-thirty," Jacinda said. "He manages pain really well."

"Get him a thousand ibruprofen," the doctor said. "He'll need it." He turned back to Reese. "Just a circuit, around the floor here. See how you do."

Reese's chest seemed to collapse. He couldn't get a proper breath, no matter how hard he tried. "I can't...breathe."

"That's the ribs," the doctor said gently. "It's okay. You're breathing fine."

But Reese didn't think so. He gasped, fought for air. Then the air filled with sand and dust and filtered sunlight. Yells rang out. Gunshots followed. His ears hurt from the noise of it all, from the constant way he couldn't get enough oxygen to breathe because of all the blasted sand in the air.

"Come on, Reese." His father's voice echoed through the Iraqi city. "One step at a time."

Reese blinked, and the hospital room came back into focus. "One step," he repeated, his voice dark, and rugged, and hoarse. He took the step, clenching his teeth against the pain in his abdomen.

He took one more, and then another. Soon enough, he'd

completed the loop around the floor, all of about two hundred yards.

"Think you can go again?" his dad asked.

"Yes," Reese said, knowing that the more he moved, the faster he'd heal. "I can go again."

As he finished his second circuit, Carly pushed her way back into the hallway. Her face—withdrawn and solemn—broke into sunshine and rainbows as her pretty pink lips curved upward.

"Look at you, Sergeant Sanders." She cocked one hip and folded her arms.

He wished she wouldn't look at him. At least not the person he was now. Yesterday morning, he'd fantasized about a future with a woman, something that hadn't crossed his mind in years.

And not just any woman. Carly Watters had starred in those thoughts yesterday, and she still did today.

*She won't want you,* a voice in his head said. *You're broken, weak, ruined.*

His heart hardened and he flattened out the smile that had been threatening to betray his feelings. He continued putting one foot in front of the other until he made it back to his room. Carly didn't follow him, and a mixture of relief and regret swam through Reese.

## 5

Carly pulled her purple car behind Reese's father's, but she didn't get out as quickly as he did. Reese didn't crack the passenger-side door. Carly had seen the look on his face at the hospital, and she didn't need her Master's degree to see, taste, feel his displeasure at her presence.

She squared her shoulders and stepped from her car. She smoothed down the stylish sweatshirt she'd bought in a boutique on Main Street, adoring the way it slid off one shoulder and gave her a feminine figure despite it's usual bulky drape. She'd paired it with a pair of jeans and a more sensible pair of shoes for helping a cowboy.

Except she wouldn't be using the word *help* around Reese. He'd made his opinions on having her help very clear.

*This is your job*, she told herself as she moved up the driveway to where Reese had his legs poking out the side of the car. His father stood in the doorway, telling Reese where to put his hand.

Carly opened the garage with the code and retrieved the wheelchair she'd found folded in the corner. She pushed it into position and braced herself behind it. Reese's father—Ryan Sanders—gave her a faint smile and a nod of thanks. He'd come into the hall as the nurse went over the prescriptions Reese had brought home and spoken with her about helping Reese.

At least she had one person on her side.

"Miss Watters has the wheelchair," Ryan said. "There you go."

Reese emerged from the car with a grimace of pain on his face. "It's so hard to breathe," he complained.

Carly's heartstrings sounded a loud note for him, but she couldn't breathe for him, much as she wanted to. She nudged the wheelchair back an inch or two so Ryan could move out of the way.

Reese refused to look at her while he shuffled the two steps to the chair, turned, and sat down. She relinquished her hold on the handles to Ryan and silently marched into the house through the garage. She had the front door unlocked and open by the time Ryan wheeled Reese up the front ramp.

"Welcome home," Ryan said cheerfully.

"Dad, I was here yesterday," Reese said, his voice barely more than a growl.

"Right." Ryan positioned Reese so he faced the television. "Well, we have pizza—supreme, pepperoni...." He glanced around.

"Salad," Carly added. "Root beer."

"Not hungry," Reese said, his fingers turning white on the armrests from his vice-grip.

"Come on," Ryan said. "Carly went to all the trouble to—"

"No one asked her to." He glared in her general direction, still refusing to make eye contact.

Carly's chest squeezed too tight, too tight. He was making her job so much more difficult than it needed to be. She didn't want to be here in Three Rivers any more than he wanted her to be. Her own fingers curled into fists as she bit back the words she'd like to say.

Ryan shrugged one shoulder as he loaded up a plate with three slices of pizza and sat heavily on the couch. "Well, I can say thank you to Miss Watters." He took a bite of pizza and swallowed it. "I can only stay for a little bit," he said, picking up the remote and switching on the TV. "You should eat. Then you can take your pill, and you'll feel better."

"I feel fine, Dad."

"But you do need to take that pill, and Carly picked up your prescriptions too."

Reese glared at his lap, then lifted his eyes to where Carly stood nervously in the kitchen. Like yesterday, she felt as if he could see more than just her clothes, her hair, but all the way into her soul. "Fine. Pepperoni. With ranch dressing. I have some in the fridge."

Carly nodded and turned away from his appraisal. She put together a plate of food for him and took it into the living room. "Root beer? Or water?"

"Oh, this kid loves the soda." Ryan chuckled. "Can you get me some, too?"

"Dad, she's not your care coordinator."

"I don't mind," Carly said. She certainly wasn't going to load up a plate with cheesy goodness and sit down like she was friends with these two men.

*This is your job. This is your job.* She recited it a few more times as she poured soda into tall glasses and collected Reese's medication, and took everything into the men. Unsure of what to do next, she pulled out her laptop and set up on Reese's kitchen table.

He didn't even glance her way. Low conversation between him and his father met her ears, but she pretended like she was so absorbed in Facebook they'd disappeared. Really, she opened a blank email and typed everything running through her mind.

Her counselor in college often advised her to do this. Quinn said it would help her discover why she was feeling a certain way —angry, nervous, worried, whatever. And right now, Carly had no idea what she was feeling or why.

As the minutes passed, though, it became clear that everything teeming inside had to do with Reese. What Reese thought of her. Why he hadn't warmed up to her, despite her driving forever to the ranch, buying him ice cream, and bringing him coffee. Why it mattered so much to her that he did acknowledge her, speak with her, like her.

"Well, I better be goin'." Ryan stretched as he stood. "It's a couple hours in that rickety sedan, and Mom'll be wondering where I am."

Reese acted like he'd get up and walk his father out. The flinch of pain stealing across his face seemed to remind him that he'd fallen off a horse and then been stomped on. "Thanks, Dad."

He accepted the embrace his dad gave him, and Ryan caught Carly's eye. She got up and slipped out the garage exit to wait for him in the driveway. Ryan stuffed his hands in his jeans pockets and examined the garage like it held a gold mine.

"He's gonna be rude to you," he said. "But please stay. I've seen him like this before, and he thinks he wants to be alone. But he doesn't. And he shouldn't be."

Carly nodded, not quite sure what to say. Besides her father's death, she'd never dealt with a tragedy so close to her. And she'd only been twelve then. All she knew was her life got turned upside down and the Watters family had started doing things differently.

Reese would learn that too. He had once before, at least.

"Okay," she said. "How long should I stay, do you think?"

"Until he kicks you out or he falls asleep."

A squeeze of fear stole the breath from her lungs. "What if he kicks me out right after you leave?"

"He won't," he said. "I told him to let you stay through dinner. Said he owed you that." He glanced toward the front door. "If Reese is one thing, it's dutiful. He'll let you stay for a while."

Carly resisted the urge to check her watch, knowing it didn't really tell time. The fashion piece suddenly felt like a pair of handcuffs around her wrist. Surprise consumed her when Ryan engulfed her in a hug. She felt small and insignificant in his arms, what with his huge physical presence and his calm demeanor.

Something inside her stuttered, and Carly stepped out of the fatherly embrace she hadn't had in her life in almost fifteen years. "Thank you, Sergeant Sanders."

"Oh, it's Ryan," he said. "And that man in there is Reese. He'll make you think he's tough and military, but he's...well, he *is* tough and military. But he has a heart too."

"Of course." Carly wasn't sure what Ryan meant, but she'd seen a glimpse of Reese's heart when he'd shown her the horses yesterday. The exterior he wore now came from pain, and embarrassment, and other things she couldn't even fathom.

Ryan lifted his hand in good-bye, and Carly faced the front door, a vibration running through her bloodstream at having to fill the hours and silence between now and dinnertime.

---

Reese fumed the longer Carly stayed outside with his father. The car's engine hadn't started yet, and he hated that they were talking about him. His phone went off over and over, messages from all his brothers, some of their wives. The group text didn't bring him peace or comfort, though it probably should. His brothers cared, but he still felt like the seventh in a long line of amazing men. Like he'd never measure up, especially now.

Finally, he heard the distant sound of an engine turning over, and some of the tension in his neck loosened. It returned in full force, though, when he realized he could no longer use his father as a buffer between himself and Carly. He wanted to talk to her as much as he wished she'd leave him alone.

She pushed open the front door at the same time she knocked on it. "Hey."

"Hey," he responded, his voice softer and kinder than he'd previously been able to make it. "You really don't have to stay."

"Your dad said I could stay until dinner." She sat on the end of the couch furthest from him. "So I'm going to do that."

He nodded, his eyes trained on his lap. The medication she'd given him had dulled the pain in his hip and back to a tolerable level, but breathing still felt like the worst kind of chore.

"Where you stayin'?" he asked.

"Some hotel...somewhere."

He glanced up to find her frowning.

"I'm not sure where it is in relation to your house. But it's way across town from the coffee house."

"Thank you for the coffee," he said, taking in the beauty of her smile when she allowed it to cross her lips. "You're wearing different clothes."

"There's a charming shop on Main Street. My credit card is a little heavier, but my wardrobe got improved." She flashed another grin, this one revealing some of the nerves she was trying to conceal.

"Tell me more about what a mirror twin means."

She hesitated, and Reese recognized the faint lines that appeared around her eyes. He wore that look when he was trying to figure out what to say, what wouldn't give too much away, how much he trusted the person listening.

"Cassie dyes her hair dark now," she finally said. "So no one knows we're twins. She's doing a biology doctorate at Washington State University."

"That has nothing to do with mirror twins," he teased.

"No, I suppose it doesn't." She finally looked at him—right at him—her expression open and vulnerable. His heart constricted and then expanded as he recognized the hurt she felt. It might not be physical, the way his mostly was, but she'd been wounded too. He wanted to know when, and by whom, and how he could make it better.

He glanced away first. "Man, it's hard to breathe with broken ribs."

"I've heard that," she said. "My sister's husband is an ER doctor."

Reese didn't have fond memories of ER doctors—or any doctors for that matter. Their coolness when delivering bad news unsettled him. "Are all your sisters married?"

"Just my older two. Cassie's seeing someone, but she just moved last fall, so it's a long-distance thing now."

"You sound like you don't think that would work."

"I don't."

Reese nodded, adding another reason to keep his emotions and desires in check. Carly lived in Amarillo, and though that wasn't as great a distance as Texas to Washington, it wasn't right around the corner either.

"You grow up in Texas?" he asked.

"Yeah. Born in Dallas, but my family moved to Amarillo when I was little. My mom still lives there."

Reese heard the catch in her voice, even if it only stumbled for one syllable. "Just your mom?"

She swallowed, and her blue eyes seemed to sharpen, brighten. "My dad died in Operation Anaconda."

A flaming fist punched Reese in his already injured lungs. "I'm so sorry," he managed to press between his lips. He knew Operation Anaconda—one of the first strikes of the war in Afghanistan, troops had tried to take a valley from the Taliban.

"I was twelve," she continued, her voice robotic. "But I still miss him."

Reese had often wondered if anyone would miss him had he died overseas. His parents, sure. But he hadn't had a wife, a girl-friend, no one significant in his life, no one counting on him to come home. "Of course you do," he said. "My mom suffers from such terrible anxiety, she can barely leave the house. Having all her sons serve in the Army like their dad really did a number on her."

Carly didn't seem surprised by his statement. Didn't seem to judge him—or his mom. "Is that why she didn't come see you in the hospital?"

Reese tried to clear the emotion from his voice before he spoke. It didn't quite work, because when he said, "Yeah. She can't handle seeing me...unwell. Anyone, really, but especially me," his voice had dropped an octave.

She let his sentence hover in the air between them. Long enough to make Reese want to say something—anything—to eradicate the last thing he'd said.

"So." He chuckled, and it sounded so nervous—and sent a sharp pain around his chest from front to back. "Tell me something about yourself that doesn't matter at all."

The tension in her jaw lessened; the lines around her eyes relaxed. "I haven't eaten a mushroom in two decades."

Reese didn't consider the pain when he threw his head back and laughed. Really laughed. He cut the sound off when he couldn't stand the ache for another second. It dulled as he grinned at her. "I don't really like mushrooms either. Maybe on pizza."

She scrunched up her face. "That just ruins a perfectly good pizza. They infect everything they touch."

Reese wished she'd move closer. Close enough for him to breathe in the scent of her skin. Close enough to reach out and touch if he dared to.

"What kind of ice cream did you buy yesterday? I'm thinking it's time for a treat and a movie."

She stood and tossed her blonde hair over her shoulder. "Thought you said you weren't going to lie around and watch TV."

He yawned. "I lied. But I'll probably fall asleep, just to warn you."

She moved into the kitchen and opened the freezer. "So, I got...peanut butter cup." She watched him for a reaction, and he applauded her choice.

"Can't go wrong with peanut butter and chocolate."

"Right?" She set the carton on the counter next to the fridge. "And lime sherbet."

Reese made a face. "Lime sherbet? Do they even make sherbet anymore?"

"Yes, Mister, they do." She opened one drawer and closed it. Opened another and closed it. She must not have really snooped around the way she said she had. She didn't even know where the silverware was.

"Drawer next to the dishwasher," he said. "I want the ice cream."

"Great," she said airily. "Leaves all the sherbet for me." She returned to the living room only a few minutes later, bearing bowls of cold treats. "So, what do you want to watch?" She eyed the bookshelf holding his movies with wariness.

"Something old, with a great soundtrack."

She set her sherbet on the coffee table and licked her spoon. Reese felt paralyzed watching her, and the thought was as horrifying as when the doctor had said the word in the hospital.

How could Carly ever see him as a man? As someone who could take care of her, provide for her, love her? He couldn't take care of himself, provide for himself, or even love himself.

Familiar bitterness and his old friend regret laced themselves through him, turning his sweet concoction into something tasteless.

"The Man From Snowy River." Carly plucked a case from the shelf and turned toward him, triumphant. "Cowboys, danger, horses." She glanced at him. "Romance."

"And good music," he added, not daring to think that the glint in her eye meant more than it did. Truth was, he had no idea what it meant. She stuck the movie into the player, grabbed the remotes from the entertainment center, and sat on the end of the couch closest to him this time.

Close enough to catch the scent of lemons, and coconut, and that lime sherbet. Close enough to reach out and touch if he were a more daring man.

But he wasn't. So he ate his ice cream, and impersonated the Australian accent of the cowboys in the movie, and fell asleep before the couple kissed, his own mind revolving around Carly Watters and if she'd let him kiss her out on the range, the way Jim kissed Jessica.

## 6

Carly woke before dawn and couldn't go back to sleep. She stayed in bed for a few minutes, ordering her thoughts. Her thoughts that revolved around Reese Sanders.

She'd stayed with him through the afternoon, even after he fell asleep during the movie. His handsome face without worry and pain had struck her like lightning, and she'd watched him instead of the feature film.

She'd made dinner, and ate it with him, and they'd talked and laughed and...bonded. Carly rolled over and opened her eyes. She couldn't believe she felt something so powerful for a cowboy. Since Tanner, she'd only dated executives, or chefs, or carpenters. But none of them had elicited the flurry of fireworks now parading through her system the way Reese had after only one day together.

With phone calls to make and time to use the hotel gym, Carly got herself out of bed. An hour later, she had appointments with two of her new cases and had put in forty minutes on the treadmill.

She showered, put on the new sundress she'd purchased at the boutique, and headed out for coffee.

Reese's house sat in sunlit silence. The peace radiating from the tranquil, small-town neighborhood pierced Carly's bubble of dislike. Maybe country life had advantages over city life, and she'd never known it. Never even tried to appreciate the simplicity of only having one choice for shopping, and one bank to run to, only a few addresses to keep track of.

The porch light switched off, and Carly startled. She grabbed the coffee and headed toward the front door. Reese had it open before she reached the steps, already dressed and wearing his taupe cowboy hat.

"Mornin'. Saw you sittin' out there."

She handed him one of the mugs. "Yeah, just thinking." She smiled as he leaned against the doorway to let her slide past. Unable to help herself, she took a deep drag of air when she was closest to him, trying to memorize the tonalities of musk and mint and man. It could've been her imagination, but she thought his chest expanded as he breathed her in too. The corners of her mouth turned up at the idea.

"You're up today," she said. "How are you feeling?"

"Better than yesterday." He gimped along behind her as she went into the kitchen. "You look great in that dress."

She turned and found him only feet away, a ruddy blush working its way up his throat into his face. Pleasure at his compliment poured through her. "Thank you, Sergeant. I like your hat."

He ducked his head and put one hand on his hat like he'd forgotten he'd put it on.

"Eat breakfast yet?" she asked.

He glanced up. "I don't eat breakfast."

"It's the most important meal of the day."

"If you're twelve." He kicked a smile in her direction, and that tether that had sprung to life the first time they met, and strengthened over their conversation yesterday, tugged tugged tugged against Carly's resolve.

"So you go to work, out on a ranch, with huge beasts, and you don't eat first?"

"Pete usually has something in the office." He looked out the window to his right. "And I don't always work with the horses."

"You don't?"

"No." He leveled his gaze at her, and she felt every inch of his Army Sergeant stare. "I'm a receptionist."

Carly flinched at the disdain in his voice. "Well, I'm a paper-pusher," she said. "Five years of school—and a Master's degree—and a bunch of student debt—so I can look at files and talk to people who wish I wouldn't." She tried to make her statement—and all it had revealed—lighter by tacking a giggle onto the end.

Regret still washed over Reese's face. "Sorry I said I didn't need you. I...do. Need your help. Need...." He focused out the window again, and he must've seen something fascinating because he steadfastly refused to look back at her. "Something," he finished.

"We all do," she said. "And I eat breakfast, so can I make some scrambled eggs?"

He waved into the kitchen, and she took that to mean *Eat whatever you want.*

She got out the eggs, milk, and butter. As she set the pan on the stove, Reese asked, "So what do you need, Miss Carly?"

She startled at the question. The question no one had asked her in a long time, maybe ever—except for him. Twice now. Her first impulse was to build a wall and shut him out. She'd known him for two days, and he didn't get to sit at the table of Carly Watters and know everything.

Except, as she whisked the eggs and milk and salt together, she thought she might have already told him everything.

"I don't know," she said.

"You have everything you want?"

"Obviously, no." She thought of the credit card payments, the student loan, the job she'd worked for but didn't know how to do, the empty apartment.

"What's obvious about that?" he asked. "Great job—"

"Paper-pusher," she reminded him.

"—nice car. Cute clothes. Those heels...." He whistled. "Maybe your family isn't perfect, but whose is?" He sat on a barstool, a whoosh of air coming out in a half-groan. "You're beautiful, and smart, and kind, and...detail-oriented."

She loved the sound of his voice as he listed her desirable qualities. But did he really feel that way about her? Did he really want to know her insecurities? The way she painted over difficult things with the right shade of lipstick, and a pair of expensive shoes, and a smile she knew turned heads?

"You barely know me," she said, her voice hardly making it past her own vocal chords.

"I know you drove out to the ranch to see me, and you weren't happy about it. But you did it."

She poured the eggs into the hot skillet, wishing he'd stop talking now, even if his baritone voice could paint beautiful pictures.

"I know you returned to Amarillo, and then came right back to Three Rivers when you heard I'd been hurt. I know you stayed with me all day yesterday, even though I wasn't very nice to you."

She turned around and leaned into the counter behind her, her eyes searching his for what he meant by all this. "So what?" she challenged. "Maybe I'm just doing my job, because I have so many bills I can't afford not to."

He stood, and even though he couldn't quite get a proper breath, and his left leg would never be as long as his right, he seemed powerful, and tall, and utterly breathtaking in that cowboy hat and with a couple days of hair on his face.

She sucked in a breath as he moved around the counter and

came toward her. The eggs needed to be stirred, but she couldn't bring herself to move.

He stopped only a foot away and looked down at her with admiration—and something more?—in his expression. "It's more than that." The quietness of his voice didn't quite match his powerful presence. "I know it is. I can feel it."

Without thinking about the message that might get sent, without considering the consequences, Carly reached up and touched the button on his chest pocket, right above his heart. "What can you feel?"

He leaned closer, the edge of his cowboy hat brushing her ear. She closed her eyes as he placed one hand on the counter at her hip.

"The point is, Carly, that I feel something." He took another breath that surely hurt his ribs. "And I didn't expect to feel this calm. The first time I was hurt, I didn't feel anything but hurt, and pain, and rage for so long."

Her fingers fisted the cloth of his shirt as if she needed him close to keep herself upright. Maybe she did. "I don't see what that has to do with me."

"You're not just doin' your job." He leaned away, stepped back, abandoned her when she wanted him to stay close. "Tell me you're not."

She opened her eyes and found him watching her with all the intensity of a nearly-broken man who could be shattered by her words.

"I'm not just doing my job," she said, feeling brave and daring and reckless. Things she never allowed herself to feel, not since her father's death had forced her to be responsible and level-headed and self-sacrificing. "I enjoyed my time with you yesterday."

She turned back to the stove, thinking the conversation over now. The scrambled eggs were ruined, and she'd just reached for the pan when he said, "Would you go out with me?"

Desire and fear collided inside Carly's mouth, rendering her mute. She left the eggs again, needing to see Reese's face, determine what he meant by the question.

"I mean, if you weren't my care coordinator," he said. "If you'd just met me at the grocery store, or at the park, and I asked you out. Would you go?"

Carly realized she hadn't told him everything. Images of Tanner danced through her mind as she tried to figure out why this mattered to Reese.

"Okay," he said, shuffling backward until he met the counter too. "You've answered."

His tormented expression, the way he hung his head so she couldn't see his eyes, spurred her into action. "No, I haven't," she said. She flipped off the stove and dumped the eggs into the sink.

"Of course I'd go out with you." She wasn't sure what to say next. She just opened her mouth and let the words out. "You're tall, dark, and handsome, and strong, and not into rodeo, right? Because my last boyfriend left me for the rodeo circuit." She cocked her hip as he met her gaze. "Kinda got me off cowboys for a while." She scanned the length of his body, as if really considering if she'd give him a chance. "But you might hook me on them again."

"I'm not into rodeo," he said. "I can barely walk."

"You walk just fine," she said.

"You don't like cowboys?"

She shook her head. "Not really. But you said you're a receptionist, so...." She shrugged, unsure where this conversation would end. "I mean, if I wasn't your care coordinator, and you didn't live in the middle of nowhere, and we'd just met at an art gallery in the city, and you asked, I'd say yes."

He blinked as that delicious blush crept into his face again. "Never been to an art gallery."

Frustration boiled through her, making her empty stomach riot. "We probably would've never met then." The thought bled sadness through her. At the same time, she couldn't go out with him. Veteran care coordinators needed to maintain a professional boundary, one she'd probably already crossed by bringing him coffee and making him dinner.

A new thought entered her mind—she needed to call Lex. Figure out how to work with these men without falling in love with one of them.

Not just one of them.

Reese Sanders.

---

REESE LET CARLY retreat inside her mind. SHE REMADE THE scrambled eggs that had turned brown during their exchange while he sat at the island with her words reverberating through his mind.

*I'd say yes.*

*Would've never met.*

*You walk just fine.*

*Tall. Dark. Handsome. Strong.*

Did she really find him strong? Him? With his limp, compromised core muscles, and broken ribs?

*You don't always have broken ribs*, he told himself. But if he really allowed himself to believe that blonde, beautiful Carly Watters would go out with him, he couldn't breathe.

"Think you can go for a ride?" she asked. "I have to meet with another client out at Courage Reins."

Apprehension blipped through him. "Courage Reins?"

"He has a riding appointment at noon, and I'm meeting with him afterward."

Reese checked the clock. "It's only nine."

"I know." She forked another bite of eggs into her mouth, and Reese ripped his eyes away from her lips. "Maybe you can show me the horses again."

He felt tired already. "Not sure I can stand that long."

"We'll take your chair."

He shook his head. "No, thanks." He didn't need Pete seeing him in a wheelchair. Or Garth. Or any of his cowhand friends, or the other clients at Courage Reins.

"Okay." She didn't push him, something he appreciated, but didn't say. She stayed a while longer, promised to be back in the afternoon to check on him, and moved toward the front door.

"I don't need you to check on me," he said. "I'll call you if I need anything."

She paused with her hand on the doorknob, her blue eyes broadcasting a storm he couldn't quite decipher. "All right. Call me later, then, Sergeant."

With those formal words, she slipped away from him. And he let her, because the alternative—getting rejected or being babysat —would be so much worse.

THAT AFTERNOON, SOMEONE KNOCKED ON THE FRONT DOOR. FROM his position in the reclined armchair, Reese glanced toward it, expecting to see Carly pushing her way in with a timid smile and a bag of fast food in her hand.

She didn't.

"Reese?" a man called.

Reese knew the voice, but took an extra moment to place it. "Come in, Pastor Scott."

The door opened, and a tall, lanky man entered. He wore regular clothes, like he'd been working in his yard that afternoon and suddenly thought to visit the wounded veteran who lived down the street from him.

"Crystal sent over some bread." He held up the paper-wrapped loaf and stepped toward the kitchen. Reese managed to get himself into an upright seated position by the time Scott returned.

"How are you doing?" The pastor sat on the couch closest to Reese, his hazel eyes kind and unassuming.

"My ribs hurt," he said. "But everything else is healing fast."

"Do you need me to get you something?"

"Nah. Just took my meds a little while ago. That's why I was napping. They sort of put me out."

Pastor Scott nodded. "Been there. Had surgery on my knee in college."

The two men sat in silence for a few heartbeats. Reese had endured dozens of surgeries to try to put his hip back together. Or at least have a hip at all. He'd swallowed his fair share of painkillers and anti-inflammatories.

"Some of the ladies set up a meal schedule," Pastor Scott said. "Miss Rosemary is bringing you something tonight."

"That's so kind," Reese said, his voice suddenly thick with emotion. He'd only lived in Three Rivers for a few years, and yet the sense of belonging felt like he'd been here forever. "But it's not necessary. My veteran care coordinator—"

"Miss Carly," Pastor Scott said. "She called me this morning. She suggested the meals."

Reese's eyebrows darted up. "She did?"

"Real nice girl," Pastor Scott continued. "Said you might could use some company in the evenings." He peered at Reese. "Miss Rosemary is bringin' her golden. She knows you love dogs."

Reese's heart felt too full, ready to overflow and choke him. "I love Honey," he said. "I'm so glad Rosemary's bringing her."

Pastor Scott stood. "Well, I can't stay long. Just wanted to check on you, let you know about the meals." He paused as he shook Reese's hand. "See you Sunday?"

"I'll try to be there," Reese promised.

An hour later, Rosemary showed up at the door with a pot of

chili, some of her famous homemade cornbread, a green salad, and her seven-year-old golden retriever, Honey.

"You sit at his feet," she admonished the dog as she took the food into the kitchen. "No jumping. The man is hurt."

Reese laughed, though the movement sent fire along his ribs. "Honey doesn't jump."

"Oh, she does when she sees you."

He whistled at the dog, and she came trotting over. He scratched her ears and under her neck, stealing her calm energy and infusing it into his troubled places. "Hey, girl."

Honey squinted her eyes closed in response.

"You hungry now, Reese-honey?"

"Yes, ma'am," he said. "Extra butter on my cornbread."

"You soldiers," she said. "It seems unfair that you have such great metabolisms."

A lot of things felt unfair to Reese, but that wasn't one of them. He banished the dark thoughts by focusing on what he had right now, right in front of him. A good dog who didn't care about his broken ribs or compromised abdominal wall. A kind friend and neighbor who probably needed the conversation and company as much as he did. A warm house against the spring wind.

A beautiful care coordinator who'd set everything up, put pieces of his life in place, and simultaneously turned his world upside down.

Rosemary brought him a plate with a bowl balanced on it, and three slices of heavily buttered cornbread on the side.

He thanked her and accepted the spoon she offered. "Why'd you bring the salad if you weren't going to give me any?"

She returned to the kitchen for her own plate, which held more green than his. "I have to eat too, young man." She took a bite of chili. "Oh, heavens. This is my best batch yet."

Reese spooned some chili into his mouth. "You're right, ma'am. Delicious."

"Plus, I thought your Carly would be here. She might like something green too."

*My Carly.*

"She's busy," he said, though her appointment at Courage Reins had surely ended hours and hours ago. He busied himself with eating so he didn't have to make another excuse. Because it wouldn't be for her. *He* was the one who said he'd call. *He* was the one who hadn't called. Carly respected his wishes, another thing he appreciated.

He finished eating, enjoyed the conversation with Rosemary about her daughter in Florida and her son in Utah. He adored the presence of Honey, and thought for the hundredth time that he needed to get a dog.

After Rosemary left, Reese reached for his phone, intending to call Carly and thank her for setting up the meals. But he couldn't bring himself to press call. He didn't trust himself not to say more than thank you, not to invite her over to watch another movie, not to ask her out for real, regardless of the consequences with her job.

Instead, he thumbed out a message: *Thank you for setting up the evening meals with my church.*

She didn't answer, and Reese fell asleep in the armchair with his phone waiting silently on his chest.

## 7

On Sunday morning, dawn broke over Three Rivers while Carly walked through the park. So much quiet, so much wide open sky, so much peace existed here. And with her mind churning with thoughts, and ideas, and worries, she appreciated the peace and quiet of the early morning. Even if it happened in a small town.

She'd been flirting with the idea of moving here since Pete had mentioned it in the hospital. Despite what she told him, her first reaction had been a violent *no*. But the more time she spent here, the more people she met, she realized Three Rivers was homey and comfortable.

The hours she'd spent out at Courage Reins, watching the therapy lessons and then meeting with her veterans had passed quickly and been enjoyable.

Reese had texted a couple of times, but she hadn't responded. She didn't know why, only that his proclamation that he'd call her if he needed her grated against her nerves. She'd spent the majority of two days with him, and him dictating when she could and couldn't come over annoyed her.

She needed to answer him, though, and soon. He'd asked her

to come pick him up and take him to church, which began at eleven. Pulling her phone from her back pocket, she typed out a message to him.

*I'd be happy to take you to church. Be there at 10:30.*

She thumbed off the words, and tried again.

*I'll be there at 10:30 to take you to church.*

She studied the words, satisfied they didn't say anything about how she felt about taking him to church. She was glad he asked—she wanted to help him *and* spend time with him—but she needed to keep their relationship professional. Especially since he didn't seem to mind opening doors in his life and then slamming them when she started to make her way inside.

She sighed, tucked her phone in her sweatshirt pocket, and tilted her head toward the clear, blue sky. *Give me patience*, she prayed. *Help Reese recover quickly.*

The wind picked up, and Carly needed to get back to the hotel and pack. She'd be leaving Three Rivers after church and heading back to Amarillo. At least for one day. Reese seemed to be surviving just fine without her, and she feared that if she stayed in Three Rivers much longer, she'd become attached to the Podunk town.

She stood and started the walk back to the hotel. Half a block before she'd arrive, her phone buzzed. Reese had texted.

*Can you come a little earlier? Maybe we can eat breakfast together.*

She smiled against her will. The man didn't eat breakfast, which morphed his invitation into something he hadn't said. What, she didn't know, couldn't quite name, because he might as easily push her away the moment she arrived.

"He's just...hurt right now," she muttered to herself as she quickened her pace. "If he wasn't, everything would be different between you."

She wasn't sure if she believed herself or not. Reese hadn't been overly fond of her touching him that first time out at

Courage Reins, nor was he eager to give her something to do to help him. Claimed he didn't need help.

*I get free breakfast at the hotel*, she messaged back.

*Then why did you come make eggs on Friday morning?*

She'd thought he could use the company, that was why she'd gone over there on Friday morning. After their heart-to-heart chat on Thursday, she'd wanted to see him again. Was that so wrong?

*Yes*, her mind whispered. Instead of answering his question, she dialed Lex, hoping her friend and mentor would be awake this early in the morning.

"Carly!" Lex's chipper voice reminded Carly of her affinity for mornings.

"Lex," she said. "Good morning."

"Oh, it doesn't sound like a good morning."

"You can tell that from three words?"

"I know you, Carly. As soon as I saw your smiling face on my screen, I knew something was wrong."

"Because I *called*?"

"Yes, dear Carly. This early in the morning, you'd text unless it was something urgent. So." She sighed happily, as if she prided herself on her Sherlock Holmes skills. "What's up?"

"Reese Sanders got hurt a couple of days ago."

Lex sucked in a sharp breath. "Is he okay?"

"He's got a couple broken ribs. Some bruises. He's going to be okay, in time."

"Oh, good news."

"Yeah." Carly couldn't quite bring herself to say why she'd really called.

"So...you called to tell me about Reese?"

"No, I want to talk about him. He's...."

"Difficult to read? Quiet? Determined?"

"Yes, all of the above." Carly wanted to add handsome to the list, but held her tongue. "He's...hot and cold with me. Allows me to help him one minute, and then shuts me out the next."

"Hmm." Lex let a few moments of silence slide by. "He's been re-injured, so he's probably thinking through what to do next with his life, wondering if he'll be able to keep his job, and what his future will look like. He's a thinker, that one."

"He has the same job. It's just a couple of ribs." Carly paced back and forth along the side of the hotel.

"It's *not* just a couple of ribs to him," Lex said. "I know Reese. I guarantee he'll be feeling the same way he did when he first came home from Afghanistan. Broken. Lost. Without hope. No prospects in women or jobs or anything. And you're there, reminding him of all his weaknesses, all his shortcomings. And—"

"Okay," Carly said.

"And," Lex continued, raising her voice. "You're beautiful, and he's probably doubly embarrassed that he's single, and alone, and now injured again."

"Lex," Carly said. "I get it."

"Be patient with him," Lex said. "Forgiving. When he reaches out, grab on. When he lets go, let him go."

Tears threatened to trickle down her cheeks. "Okay, Lex. Thank you. How's the job going in Denver?"

Lex spoke of her new role in the National Social Care system with such vibrancy that Carly couldn't help smiling as she went up to her room. Once she hung up with her friend, Carly sent a message to Reese.

*Packing now. Be there in twenty minutes.*

---

REESE WAITED IN THE FRONT DOORWAY, SCANNING THE STREET FOR Carly's purple car. He hated that she was packing and leaving Three Rivers, but he hadn't given her a reason to stay. He'd said he'd call if he needed help, but he hadn't been able to bring himself to do it.

He didn't *need* help.

He needed company, and the dinners she'd spurred into existence had provided some relief from his loneliness. The truth was, he wanted Carly's company but didn't know how to get it without inventing a reason for her to come over.

The tightness in his chest dissipated when she pulled into his driveway. He pushed open the screen door, but didn't step onto the porch. He wasn't sure he could. He didn't want her to push him into the chapel, but he'd told Pastor Scott he'd be at church today, and he needed the spiritual relief for his soul.

"Mornin'," he said, drinking in her black skirt and flowery blouse. It was the same outfit she'd worn out to the ranch last Wednesday, and he admired her as much now as he had then.

She approached slowly, her heels seeming to wobble under her weight. "Good morning." She lifted a brown paper sack. "I brought breakfast. Last time I tried to cook over here, it was sort of a disaster."

Reese frowned, wondering which part was a disaster. The cooking? Or the conversation?

"I brought bagels and bananas, and some of those cinnamon rolls." She ascended the steps. "So you can stop frowning. I know you eat carbs."

"I wasn't frowning over the food." Reese kept his gaze locked on hers as she stopped in front of him.

"Oh?"

"You look nice." He said the first thing that popped into his mind, wishing he could make nice into beautiful or gorgeous or breathtaking. They'd all be true.

"Thank you." She scanned his navy slacks and white shirt. "No tie for church?"

"Don't like things around my neck," he said. "I'll put it on right before we go. We've got hours still."

"Mm." She nodded at the distance over his shoulder. "Can I come in? Or are you going to block the doorway until it's time to go?"

He stumbled back, gripping the edge of the door for support. A long curl tickled his arm as she passed, and a shiver squirreled down his spine. "Carly?"

She paused in her movement toward the kitchen. She leaned her hip against the couch and peered at him. "Yeah?"

"Thank you for coming."

"Of course."

"Thank you for calling my pastor and setting up meals and visits."

She blinked. "Just doin' my job." She turned away, but not before the spikes in her voice speared him right through the heart.

He limped after her and plucked a cinnamon roll from the spread she'd laid on the counter. "I'm sorry," he said. "I did it again."

"Did what again?"

"Treated you badly." He stuffed half the roll into his mouth so he couldn't say anything else.

"It's okay." She deflated as she sat on a barstool across the island from where he stood. "I understand."

He swallowed. "That makes one of us."

"You're hurt," she said. "You're probably feeling vulnerable, and hating that I'm here and reminding you that you need help when you don't, and—"

He held up his hand and she silenced. "Can we talk about something else?"

"Sure."

He asked her about the other veterans, and how Courage Reins looked, and if she liked Three Rivers. He detected something strange in her voice when she spoke of the town, but he didn't press the issue.

Soon enough, the time for church arrived. He sat in his wheelchair and let Carly get him to the car and then into the pews. It was almost like arriving on her arm, but also miles away. Reese decided he didn't care. Everyone in Three Rivers knew about his injury, and he didn't have anything to prove to them.

No, he had everything to prove to Carly. So when Rosemary stopped by and gave him a hug, he grinned. As person after person shook his hand, and said they were glad to see him out of the house, and asked him how he was doing, his spirits lifted.

"You're popular," Carly said from beside him.

"Small town. Everyone's in everyone else's business."

"Hmm."

The service started, and Reese focused on the pastor at the front of the chapel. He spoke about God's love for His children, and how He needed each of them in the congregation to act as His hands.

"Comfort those who need it. Serve those around us, even through small acts of kindness."

Reese agreed with the pastor's sermon, grateful for those who had taken time to put together soups and stews, to bring him pizza from his favorite joint, and to spend an hour with him. Little things he hadn't given much thought to previously, but that now meant a great deal to him.

Pastor Scott continued to say that the Lord put people in our lives when we need them. Reese stiffened at this twist. He believed the pastor, which meant he believed that Carly Watters had been introduced into his life for a reason.

Reese mulled over the words of the sermon during lunch with Carly. She could open a refrigerator and make a meal out of whatever she found. She acted more like her usual, chatty self following church. Her voice had regained its normal chipper quality, and she slid him more smiles than he'd seen in a week.

"Did you like church?" she asked as they finished their open-faced turkey sandwiches. He hadn't had enough bread to make anything more, and he'd already made a mental note to ask her to take him to the grocery store. His mind circled around how he could say he needed to get out, exercise his legs. Anything to show her he did appreciate her help.

"Sure," he said. "Always have." He saw her dubious expression. "Okay, fine. Maybe I skipped a time or two when I was a teenager."

She laughed. "I think I skipped whole years when I was younger."

"Do you normally attend services in Amarillo?"

"Sometimes," she hedged. "If I'm feeling up to it."

Reese wasn't sure what that meant, and he didn't know how to ask. She seemed perfectly healthy, completely able to go to church every week without a problem. She chewed her fingernails on one hand while the others beat out a rhythm on the table between them.

With a flash of recognition, he realized Carly's injuries weren't physical, but emotional. She seemed anxious at the moment, and he wondered if she suffered from depression or had panic attacks the way he had when he'd come home from war, three years ago.

"I understand that," he said.

"You understand what?" she asked.

"Not feelin' up to doing things."

"Sometimes I just don't want to talk to anyone. You know?" She studied him with desperation in her eyes, almost begging him to know exactly what she meant.

He wished he didn't, wished she didn't feel that way. "Oh, I know."

She glanced out the window behind him. "Can we go for a walk?" She startled and a healthy pink stained her cheeks. "I mean, if you're up to it."

He braced his hands against the tabletop. For Carly Watters, he wanted to be up for anything. "Sure. Let's go."

Once free from the house, Carly sighed and tucked her arm in his. "Don't let me fall."

"Never," he vowed, his tone too serious to play off as nothing.

She didn't seem to notice. "It's so peaceful here. So quiet."

"That's why I moved here."

She didn't answer, and Reese didn't need her to. A few minutes later, as they neared the end of his block, she sniffled. The muscles in Reese's body seized, and froze.

"You okay?" He didn't dare look at her, wanting to spare her feelings.

"No," she said. "I think I have to move here."

Joy spiked through him, as strong as any drug. "And that's bad?"

"Yes." She slapped his bicep, drawing his attention to her. Thin trails of tears trickled over her cheeks. "I hate small towns."

Reese frowned again, unable to comprehend how anyone could hate Three Rivers. "Well, that is bad then."

"It's not," she said, releasing him to swipe at her face. "I felt it in church. Felt like the right thing to do was to move here, be where God wants me to be. See who I'm supposed to help."

"You can help me," Reese said, real quiet, like he didn't even want to admit it to himself. "The Lord puts people where they're supposed to be, right?"

"And everything happens for a reason." She smiled brightly up at him, but his insides went icy. Tendrils of cold spread through him as an old question—one that had plagued him for months after the bombing overseas—returned.

"And what reason would God have for shattering my hip?" he asked. "Or letting me fall off that horse?" Familiar fury licked up his chest, and old resentment flared to life.

"I didn't mean—"

"Forget it." Reese turned and headed back to his house, angry at himself for putting yet another wedge between him and Carly. Furious at God for allowing him to be in the wrong place at the wrong time. Absolutely irate that he felt this way—again—after working so hard for so long to overcome the negative thoughts.

---

REESE WOKE THE NEXT MORNING, HIS MOOD FOULER THAN THE previous day. He stayed in bed—or rather, on the couch where he'd slept—and thought about what he should be doing this Monday morning.

The annual round-up. The week-long trip had been one of the highlights of Reese's year, and he was missing it because of this stupid injury.

He let his thoughts wander past Tom, one of his best friends. He missed Tom with a fierceness he didn't know he could feel for someone who wasn't in his unit. A hole had existed in his chest since the general controller left last year, headed back to his dad's side in Montana.

He missed seeing Rose—now Tom's wife—and her daughter, Mari. They'd been such good friends, real friends he could trust with his pain, his secrets.

His physical pain seemed to pale in comparison to the abyss his mind and memories had become. So much had changed, though Tom and Rose had been gone for almost nine months. Still, Reese wished he was riding Arrowhead, the steady and sure pony that had transported him across acres and acres of the ranch as they collected the herd from the wintering grounds.

He finally got up and got himself showered, the ache of missing the annual round-up never quite settling into silence.

## 8

A week passed. Then two. Carly sold her lease in Amarillo and moved to Three Rivers, employing the help of Pete and his cowhands to help her move into a small house only a block from her beloved coffee shop.

As she drove out to the ranch on a sunny, mid-May Monday morning, she couldn't help singing along to the radio. The only stations she could find out here played country music, and surprisingly, she didn't hate it. Some of the tunes were even catchy enough to stick in her head for the day.

She'd seen Reese often, but they didn't share anything beyond the superficial. No deep confessions about a dead father, or an anxiety-ridden mother. No philosophical or religious talk. After she'd had some time to reflect on what she'd said, she'd realized how cruel it sounded. How she'd said that God had hurt Reese, instead of protecting him.

She wanted to apologize, but she didn't know how. Reese never brought it up again. Never asked her to take him to church again. She hadn't been in town anyway, except for yesterday, but she hadn't gone to church.

Wasn't feeling up to it. Up to seeing him, if she were being honest.

"But you'll see him today," she muttered as she turned from asphalt onto gravel. Reese was coming back to work today after two and a half weeks off. That was the same reason Carly was headed out to Three Rivers Ranch and Courage Reins.

He hadn't asked her to come. But Lindsay had. Lindsay had approved Carly's request to move to Three Rivers, to help Reese, to establish a way to meet with all her veterans after their equine therapy.

Carly had spent the last week making arrangements with Pete and then her veterans, packing her apartment, and moving. She still had boxes from floor to ceiling in her dining room, but she didn't care. She ate on the couch, in front of the TV, alone. No need for a dining room table.

Because of the heaviness of her heart, she switched off the radio and rolled onto the ranch in silence. She pulled her car into the end spot in the Courage Reins parking lot, noting the presence of Reese's truck, and gathered her wits. If ever there was a time to be professional, this was it. No one in the office could see her feelings for Reese. Even with the increased distance, they burned as hot and bright as ever. The simple thought of him pushed her pulse into pounding.

Someone knocked on the passenger side window, and Carly yelped. When she recognized Reese, she rolled the window down.

"You gonna sit out here all day?" he asked, leaning down to speak through the low opening.

"No," she said. "Some of us just need a few extra seconds to gather their thoughts." She unbuckled her seat belt and cut the engine.

"Window's down," he said.

She rolled her eyes. "Well, get out of the way, Sergeant."

A deep chuckle met her ears as he stepped back and she

restarted the car. It seemed as though Reese would be warm today. But Carly knew he could switch to Frosty the Snowman in less time than it took to blink.

She rolled up the window and reached for her briefcase, giving Reese plenty of time to resume his position behind the counter inside the building. But he waited for her on the sidewalk, sporting that luscious cowboy hat, a pair of jeans, and a shirt the color of butter that pulled across his broad chest.

"Mornin'."

"You should know that I dislike mornings." She stepped onto the sidewalk where he waited, right into his personal space. He didn't move back to give her any room, and she almost toppled backward. His steady hand on her arm kept her from falling. At least physically. Tingles ran up to her shoulder and down to her fingertips.

"Careful," he said.

She stared at his tanned skin against her pale forearm. He removed his fingers, cleared his throat, and stepped back.

"Pete said you'd show me where I could set up my office," she said.

"Right. Yes, I can." He gestured down the sidewalk to the entrance of the building. "Right this way, Miss Carly."

She matched her pace to his, chastising herself for falling under the charm of her name in his voice in less than two seconds. So it came out smooth, with enough emotion for her to know he cared about her. He certainly didn't act that way all the time.

She stalled before they reached the door. "Look, Reese, I just need to say something before we go in."

"Okay, shoot."

"I'm really sorry about what I said after church a couple of weeks ago. It was insensitive, and unkind, and—"

His eyes flashed a warning for her to stop, but she couldn't. Wouldn't.

"Of course I don't think the Lord injured you on purpose. Nor do I believe you did anything wrong to warrant the kinds of things you've been through." Her chest heaved for the lack of oxygen, and she took a deep breath. The scent of earth, and cows, and sunshine came with the air.

"Just like I didn't do anything to make my dad die. Sometimes things just happen." She pulled at the hem of her blouse. "So I'm sorry." She rested her fingertips on his crossed arms. "Really sorry. Can we go back to being friends? I liked that so much better than what we've been doing for the past several days."

His eyes narrowed, and she suspected she'd said something else to upset him. "Friends?" he asked.

"Anything would be better than talking about the weather or what brand of toothpaste you want." Frustration accompanied her words. "We used to discuss meaningful things. I miss that."

*I miss you.* The words twitched against the tip of her tongue.

"I miss you," she said, releasing them and hoping she hadn't said too much.

"You miss me." He didn't form the words into a question, and Carly plowed ahead.

"And I need a small town tour guide. I can't find anything here. Is Main Street really the only option for shopping? There has to be someone here who can cut my hair that isn't over the age of sixty."

Reese held her gaze for one, two, three terrifying heartbeats before he burst into laughter. He offered her his arm, which she gladly took. "I'll be your tour guide, Miss Carly. But only if you'll do somethin' for me."

She rolled her eyes as he opened the door for her. "I do everything for you."

"Something not job-related." He followed her into the building and let the door settle closed. "I want to go to the Tulip Festival next week. And I want you to come with me. Not as my veteran care coordinator. Not as my friend."

Her heart thundered as she waited for him to continue. He leaned closer, closer, until his cowboy hat brushed her earlobe. "But as my date."

She closed her eyes and absorbed the husky tone of his voice, basked in the masculine smell of his skin and clothes.

Oh, how she wanted to say yes.

So she did.

———

REESE CONTAINED HIS SMILE AFTER CARLY SAID YES TO HIS invitation to the Tulip Festival. "I'm real sorry I got so angry," he said. "That wasn't fair to you, and you didn't say anything wrong. Not really." He scrubbed the bit of hair below his hat on the back of his head. "It's just...an old hurt. One I thought I'd gotten over, but that rears up from time to time."

Truth was, feeling grateful instead of resentful required daily practice. With his injury, Reese hadn't done as well as he usually did. Being alone for twenty-three hours a day hadn't helped. Being so near Carly but unable to really tell her how he felt hadn't either. So when she'd said everything happened for a reason, he'd snapped.

He'd regretted it. Thumbed out two dozen texts to her over the past couple of weeks. Sent none of them. Muddled through each day. Called her for rides to the doctor, or the grocery store, or the post office. Nothing of consequence had been exchanged between them, and he hated it as much as she seemed to.

"When is the Tulip Festival?" she asked, drawing him out of his mind.

"Next weekend." He moved toward the left of the receptionist counter. Her office sat down the hall, second door on the left. Just out of sight of his position at the counter, but she hadn't left his mind since the morning he'd met her.

"What does one wear to a Tulip Festival?"

"Jeans and a T-shirt." He glanced at her floor-length skirt and frilly, lacy blouse. "Do you actually own any T-shirts?"

She glanced at her clothes like they'd wronged her. "I'm sure I do. I'll have to unpack to find them, though."

"I can come help you unpack."

"You have three broken ribs."

"It's been almost three weeks," he shot back. "I'm feeling great."

"The doctor said six before you can lift anything heavier than ten pounds."

"Do your clothes weigh more than ten pounds?" He cocked an eyebrow at her. He fingered her airy blouse. "This feels like cotton candy. Light as a feather."

She jerked her arm away from his fingers with a girlish giggle that sent shivers down to his toes. He wanted her to laugh like that again and again. Preferably after he kissed her.

"I don't want you unpacking my clothes," she said with an edge of darkness in her voice.

"Maybe your towels, then," he said. "I've gotta do *something*. I'm tired of sitting around my house night after night."

"Maybe my towels. Now, where's my office?" She glanced up at him, and her easy forgiveness, her effortless acceptance of him nearly undid his rigid composure. He longed to take her in his arms and kiss her.

Instead, he moved down the hall and opened the door. "It's all we've got open. It has a window."

She glanced out the glass briefly before stepping past him and into the small room. Pete had moved a desk into it late last night, after calling Reese to confirm Carly would need one.

"Desk. Chair. Window." Carly set her bag on the desk. "It'll work just fine. Ooh, look, a filing cabinet." She sat in the chair behind the desk. "Every paper-pusher needs a filing cabinet."

Reese laughed and leaned in the doorway. He didn't want to go back to his desk, where piles upon piles of papers and appointments and receipts needed to be taken care of. Pete had done the best he could in Reese's absence, but the man was a better horseman than a secretary.

What that said about Reese, he didn't know. "Well, I better get to work. I have a lot of paper to push around myself after being gone so long."

"Go on, then." She pulled out her laptop and cracked open the lid. Reese reluctantly resumed his work at his own station, the gentle elevator music his only companion.

But Carly sat only feet away, and that fact kept Reese on-edge all morning.

———

"FRIDAY NIGHT POKER," PETE SAID BY WAY OF GREETING AS HE entered the building. "You in?"

"Yeah." Reese hadn't spent much time with Pete or Garth the way he usually did. He hadn't been out in the stables or the horse barn. And though Tom Lovell had moved to Montana almost a year ago, Reese still missed his quiet presence with the horses.

"Great." Pete knocked on the counter. "Squire can't wait to hear about Miss Carly."

Reese rolled his eyes and focused back on the computer screen in front of him. He'd very nearly caught up entering the bookings Pete had scratched onto any scrap of paper he could find. He'd listened to all the voicemail messages yesterday, made all the return phone calls, and deleted their inbox. It had taken Reese a full day of work to do just that.

Courage Reins was thriving, something that brought him happiness. He paused after entering an appointment for a teenage boy who'd been to a behavioral unit twice, his thoughts wandering to the horses. He still hadn't been out to see Peony, or Tabasco, or Elvis.

He clipped together the appointments that still needed to be entered, stood, and went outside. He thought about asking Carly to come with him, but one of her veterans was due to arrive for his appointment in only a few minutes.

She didn't like the horses anyway. But Reese did. One step into the horse barn, and the nostalgia hit him like a freight train. The scent of hay, and oats, and horseflesh met his nose, and he took a long breath. His lungs filled all the way, with only a stitch of pain along his right side. Carly had refused his help with her unpacking, despite his best efforts to tell her he felt almost whole.

Truth was, he wasn't whole, and she somehow knew it, the way Peony and Hank did. He meandered down the row of stalls until he came to Peony's. She stood waiting for him, her eggshell-colored coat gleaming with a fresh brush-down.

Her eyes closed halfway as she pushed her nose into his shoulder. "Hey, girl." He stroked her cheeks and neck, feeling the disquiet in him wisp into nothing. He collected a handful of sugar cubes, which he fed to Peony and Hank, before heading back into the sunshine. Back to his desk job. Back to answering phones and entering therapy appointments.

---

"COME IN, COME IN." KELLY WAVED TO HIM AS HE GAINED THE TOP stair and inched onto the deck. He'd walked from the office building, and then climbed those fifteen steps, and his right leg felt slightly numb while his lungs labored for oxygen.

He darkened the doorway as she set out a huge tray of crackers, with four square bowls of dip behind them. She nudged bottled water and soda cans out of the way, and poured a huge bag of candy into a bowl.

Satisfied with her work, she came around the counter. "Reese, how are you?" She embraced him easily, and his tension decreased by another notch.

"I'm good, Miss Kelly." He stepped back. "Where are the other boys?"

"Oh, Squire's showing them his new toy." She rolled her eyes and laughed. "They went down to the shed real quick."

"What new toy?" Reese couldn't make it to the shed and back right now, but he couldn't help feeling left out.

"It's a riding lawn mower," she said. "Men and their power tools." She headed down the hall. "I'm going to get Finn to bed. Enjoy your game, Reese."

Kelly's cheerfulness only served to remind Reese of Carly. Difference was, Kelly was truly happy and content, while Reese suspected Carly's enthusiasm for certain things was a façade.

He lifted a bottle of water and unscrewed the cap just as he heard voices and footsteps outside. Squire, Pete, and Garth entered the house, talking about horsepower and speed and the turning radius of the new lawnmower.

"Reese." Garth clapped him on the shoulder. "How are the ribs?"

"Better and better every day." Reese took a long drink of water. "Hey, thanks for letting me sit with you and Juliette at church last week."

"Anytime, Sergeant."

Squire took a paper plate and started filling it with snacks and candy from the counter. "Come on, boys. This night's not gettin' any younger."

Reese joined their chatter about everything and nothing as he filled his own plate. He sat in the last spot at the table, and Pete shuffled the cards. While dealing the first hand, he said, "Heard you're takin' Miss Carly to the Tulip Festival next weekend."

Reese yanked his eyes from his spinach artichoke dip. "Heard from who?"

"Miss Carly herself." Pete sent him a wicked grin—and a two of clubs. Both items Reese would like to return.

"Well, I guess it's true, then."

"You like her?" Squire asked. "She's the woman who drives the purple car, right?"

"She's cute," Garth said as he picked up his last card. "Pete, you're a terrible dealer. You gave me nothin'." He tossed the cards down and glared in Pete's direction.

"Great poker face," Pete said, and relief filled Reese that he didn't have to answer about Carly while the two traded jabs.

"Juliette and I will be at the Tulip Festival," Garth said as if the conversation had never moved on. "We could walk around together. If you want."

"That's a good idea," Pete said. "Sometimes it's easier on the first date to have another couple to help with the conversation."

"Could be a bad idea," Squire said as he raised the ante. "Can't kiss 'er if you've got people with you."

Reese's face heated. "I'm not going to kiss her."

"No?" Pete asked at the same time Squire and Garth both asked, "Why not?"

"Can we talk about somethin' else?" Reese growled as he added his candy to the pot.

"Definitely not," Squire said. "Call." He threw his cards on the table in front of him. The conversation stalled as he studied everyone's cards. "You win, Reese."

"Great." Reese pulled the pile of M&M's and Reese's Pieces toward him. "Guess I should quit while I'm ahead."

"You're not leaving," Pete said. "We haven't heard anything about why you're not going to kiss Miss Carly."

"Because, Lieutenant, it's our first date."

Garth picked up the cards and shuffled them, his eyes never leaving Reese's. "People kiss on the first date."

"Yeah?" Reese challenged. "When did you kiss Juliette?"

"We're not talkin' about me." He flipped cards to each man, the chore suddenly taking all his concentration. Satisfaction flowed through Reese.

"Way I heard it, it was—"

"Not the first date," Garth practically yelled over Pete as he stared him down. "I know. But you and Miss Carly have already been spending a lot of time together."

"It's a work relationship for her," he said.

"Doesn't mean it can't be something more." Squire picked up his cards. "I know all about that. But kiss 'er at the Tulip Festival, Sergeant. No one wants their first kiss to be on a ranch."

"They don't?" Pete asked, his voice slightly higher than normal.

Squire shot a surprised look at Pete. "Don't tell me...." He glanced around. "Where'd you kiss my sister?"

Pete whistled as he buried his face behind his cards.

"The barn?" Squire guessed.

Pete smiled and shook his head.

"Backyard?" Garth asked, joining the game.

Reese added his voice to the choir—"Hay fields?"—to keep the spotlight off of him and his forthcoming date with Carly. By the time he left Squire's house, his heart felt lighter than it had in weeks.

arly pushed her shopping cart up and down the aisles at Vince's grocery store, wishing another option existed for the rice noodles she'd found. But the package she had in the cart had been way down on the bottom shelf as it was, almost hidden behind the sesame oil.

She supposed not many people in Three Rivers appreciated Thai food, but her frustration remained. The town seemed to have plenty of places to eat out, a fact she appreciated as she stopped by a different establishment most evenings after work.

Doing so kept her from going to Reese's and spending the time with him. She'd eat her Chinese, or her Italian sub, or her pizza while she steadily worked through the boxes. She almost had everything unpacked now, an accomplishment she couldn't wait to brag to someone about. If only there were someone to tell.

"Hey, there."

She glanced away from the narrow selection of organic vegetables and found a tall man standing beside her with a couple of apples in his large hands.

"Hello." She re-focused on the spring greens.

"You new in town?"

"Yeah, just moved here last weekend." She made her selection —half baby spinach, half spring greens—and started to move away.

"I'm Tyler," he said, dropping the apples and following her. "I'm new in town too."

Something inside her paused. "Oh yeah? What brings you out to Three Rivers?"

Tyler wore the standard jeans and T-shirt, with cowboy boots —a definite strike. But he wasn't sporting a cowboy hat.

"I just started out at the ranch." He sounded mighty proud of himself.

"Oh, maybe I'll see you out there, then," she said. "I'm a social worker stationed at Courage Reins."

A smile took up his whole face. "That's great, but maybe I can see you this weekend...." He shuffled those booted feet and looked around the produce section. But on a Friday night, the audience was pretty bare. "We can go to dinner or something."

Carly's immediate thought centered around Reese. "I can't." She grabbed the first bunch of broccoli her hands touched and didn't bother to bag it before dropping it in her cart. "I'm busy at work and I'm still unpacking." She flashed him a fake smile to take the sting out of her rejection.

"Maybe next weekend, then." Tyler followed her past the root vegetables.

Carly wanted to get out of produce, get out of the grocery store. "I already have a date next weekend." That stopped him from following her, and a pang of regret touched her heart. "There's a Tulip Festival. You should ask someone else to go. Or just go yourself. You might meet someone there." She gave him a real smile this time, and he lifted his hand in a wave.

Carly drove home and poured herself a bowl of cold cereal instead of making the Thai beef and broccoli she'd been planning. Her phone rang, and a flash of happiness stole through her when she saw Reese's face.

Just as quickly as that had come, a wave of anxiety hit her. "Reese?" she answered. "Are you okay?"

He chuckled. "Of course I'm okay."

She grated against the words of course. "Well, you never call if you're okay," she said. "In fact, you never call."

A sigh came through the line. "Yeah, sorry about that. Wondered what you were doin' tonight."

She glanced down at her empty bowl of cereal, her heart shrinking inside her chest. "Unpacking."

"Surely you're almost done with that."

She didn't tell him she'd only done one box, maybe two, each night before spending the rest of her evening in front of the television. "Getting there."

"Can you leave it for one night? I want to show you the town."

A smile thinned her lips. "Take me out for a night on the town?"

He cleared his throat. "Well, it's not like we can go clubbing or anything. But there's karaoke at the sports bar."

Carly's throat closed. Tanner had always wanted to hang out in sports bars on Friday nights. "I don't sing, and I don't like sports bars."

"Thank the stars," he said, exhaling as he spoke. "I don't either."

Curiosity crept through her, and she couldn't keep the flirtatious tone from her voice when she asked, "Then why'd you suggest going there?"

She breathed in, and out. In, and out.

"I just want to see you," he finally said. "I don't care what we do."

She ducked her head, like he was there and could see her. Could see the blush heating her face. Could see the desire to see him in her eyes. Could see how much his words pleased her.

"Not sure how far I can walk," he added. "It's been a busy week."

"A movie, then?" she suggested. "There's a theater here, right?" She thought she'd seen a sign advertising showtimes, but she couldn't remember where.

"Yeah, down by that coffee shop you like."

"Perfect," she said. "You want to come get me? Or meet there? Or I can swing by and pick you up."

"I'll come get you. What's your address?"

---

Nerves battled themselves inside Reese's body as he walked up to Carly's front door. As he held open the passenger-side door for her to climb into his truck. As he paid for the movie tickets, and bought popcorn and soda and Junior Mints for the beautiful woman hanging onto his arm like *she* needed *him* to stay upright.

She wore a pink and blue striped tank top paired with a pair of jean shorts. Her flat sandals made him a good six inches taller than her, despite his injuries.

He exhaled as they settled into the seats in the front row of the upper section. At least he hadn't used his wheelchair.

"You're tired," she commented before tossing a few kernels of popcorn into her mouth.

"Yeah. Sorry."

"You don't have to be sorry for being tired."

He reached for a handful of popcorn too, wishing she would so he could touch her. Having her so close, with the smell of her perfume wafting with the salt and butter of the popcorn, pushed him closer and closer to saying and doing something he wouldn't be able to take back.

*You already asked her out*, he told himself as the theater darkened and the previews began. *She already said yes.*

He wasn't even sure what they'd chosen to watch. Reese normally planned outings, how long they'd take, how much they'd cost, when he'd be home. But tonight had become an adventure from the moment he'd dialed Carly.

She'd chosen the movie that was starting next, and he'd passed over his debit card without asking how much anything cost. Truth was, he didn't care what played on the screen in front of him, or how much a tub of movie theater popcorn would set him back. He just wanted to be in the same place as Carly.

The movie started, and she passed the container of popcorn to him and lifted her drink to her lips. She placed the cup on her left-hand side, and Reese sucked in a breath and decided to be brave.

He lifted the armrest between them and drew her into his side. She tucked her shoulder under his arm and snuggled in, laying her cheek directly over his heartbeat. He half-hoped she couldn't feel how it had suddenly exploded into a rapid-fire beat. At the same time, maybe his pulse could tell her everything he wanted her to know. Maybe his body could say what his mouth hadn't been able to.

---

THE NEXT SEVERAL DAYS SHOWED REESE WHAT KIND OF LIFE HE could enjoy with Carly. They sat next to each other at church, meandered down the sidewalk to the picnic, and saw each other at work. He'd taken to eating his lunch in her office, and she'd suggested they drive out to Courage Reins together.

She arrived in his driveway on Thursday morning, and Reese muttered instructions to himself. Instructions for what to say, and how to act, and what not to say, and how not to act. He hadn't kissed her after the movies, though he'd wanted to. He'd held her hand on the way to the picnic, but there'd been no kissing then either.

And he certainly wasn't going to lay one on her while they carpooled to work. Squire and Pete and Garth's words echoed in his head. He wouldn't kiss her on the ranch, but all signs pointed at a kiss at the Tulip Festival.

He might combust if he didn't kiss her soon.

"The Tulip Festival," he whispered to himself as he descended the steps without using the ramp. She didn't get out and greet him, but grinned as he made his way around the front of her car.

"I don't think I'm going to fit in this," he said after opening the door.

"Just fold yourself in, Sergeant."

He did, after moving the seat as far back as it would go. He fit just fine, and she reached over to flip the car into gear. After backing out, she reached for his hand. He gave it to her willingly, a burst of happiness diving through him that she had initiated the contact.

The talk was small on the way to work, and she maintained her professional distance as they entered the building. He got to work to distract himself from marching into her office and kissing her right then.

Veterans came and went. Doors opened and closed. Reese answered phones, and balanced accounts, and waited for the clock to say it was lunchtime. His calendar popped up a reminder that he and Pete needed to submit their annual grant to keep their PATH International status.

Along with that, several other grants—including the one that paid Reese's salary—needed to be renewed by July first. With only fifteen days until the forms needed to be submitted, Reese sent a text to Pete, asking him to come over for a meeting about the grants by Friday.

*After lunch today?* he messaged back.

*See you then.* Reese stood and moved to the mini-fridge under the end of the counter. A door down Carly's hall opened and closed, and bootsteps echoed against the tile. Reese didn't think anything of it until he started toward Carly's office. He stalled when he heard a masculine voice speaking.

"...dinner tomorrow night?"

Reese's heart flopped around in his chest like a fish out of water. He recognized the voice. It belonged to Ethan Greene. Whole, strong, masculine Ethan Greene.

Carly's lighter, feminine tone met his ears, but he couldn't make out the words.

Ethan responded, but the roar in Reese's ears drowned out anything else. The blond cowboy walked in front of the desk, and Reese couldn't tell from his walk if Carly had said yes or not.

Surely she hadn't. She'd snuggled into *him* at the movies last Friday. She'd held *his* hand on the way to the picnic—and this very morning, hours ago. But he hadn't kissed her. Hadn't solidified their relationship. Hadn't even defined it.

He gripped his lunchbox in his fist and stepped toward her office, feeling a rush of courage fill him from top to bottom. He'd define it right now.

## 10

"What did Ethan Greene want?" Reese stood in her doorway, his lunchbox paying the price of his frustration.

So he'd heard Ethan ask her out. She'd wished Ethan would've kept his voice down, but she'd handled the situation with him, the same way she had with Tyler at the grocery store.

"Wanted me to go to dinner with him tomorrow night." She gestured toward the chair opposite her desk. He moved toward it, and she appreciated his candor, the way he wore his jealousy and displeasure right on his face.

"What'd you say?"

"I told him I was busy tomorrow night." She pulled her lunch out of her drawer. "So don't make a liar out of me. Where are you taking me tomorrow night?"

Reese's surprise was almost cute. Almost. Hadn't she made her feelings for him clear? She'd held the man's hand for forty minutes on the way to work this morning. She was risking her whole existence to be with him. Her job. Her new life in Three Rivers. Everything.

"Carly—"

An earthquake of doubt shattered her confidence. "Reese, if you tell me you can't go out with me tomorrow night, I...." Tears pressed behind her eyes, and she pushed against them with all the force she had. "You realize I'm risking a lot, right?"

"I wasn't going to say no." He set his lunch on the floor. "I know what you're risking."

"Do you? Because as soon as I tell my boss that I'm involved with you, it's over. I won't have a job." She looked away, but didn't have anything to focus on. Her gaze came back to his handsome face, his caring concern. "I won't have a reason to stay in Three Rivers."

"*I'm* in Three Rivers. You're my veteran care coordinator. I need you here."

She sniffed, wishing her emotions didn't live so close to the surface. "I need a paycheck, Sergeant."

His steady gaze never left hers. "I have an idea about that."

"Let's hear it."

"We have to renew the grants next month. I'm going to talk to Pete about putting you on the staff at Courage Reins. You won't need your social work job. You can work with all the veterans right here."

His words sent shock waves through her. Shock waves strong enough to force her back into her chair. "Really?"

"I just need a number for the grant," he said. "A fair salary for someone with your qualifications."

Her mind spun, first from his proposal, then to what kind of salary she could get, and back to Reese's quiet strength and extraordinary good looks. "I'll get you a figure later today."

He grinned and picked up his food. "Great."

*Yeah, great,* Carly thought as she bit into her apple. She needed to tell Lindsay about her relationship with Reese. She knew it was better to be up-front about such things, but she couldn't stomach the thought of not having a job only two weeks after she'd uprooted her life. She could wait a little longer.

Another glance at Reese, and she knew he could be worth it.

———

THE TINKLING BELL ON THE DRESS SHOP DOOR BROUGHT A SENSE OF calmness to Carly's psyche. Shopping had always soothed her, and though she didn't have much money, she'd determined that morning that she also didn't have anything suitable to wear to the Tulip Festival with Reese that afternoon.

"Carly." Andrea Larsen, the shop's owner stepped out from behind the counter. "Come to spend your twenty percent off coupon?"

Carly held up the slip of paper. "I need something cute for the Tulip Festival. A top." She poked around the racks closest to the door, letting Andrea look near the back. The distance between them didn't stop her from chattering.

"If I remember right, you like bright colors."

"Maybe I should go with something more subdued." She fingered the sleeve of a gray tunic. "The flowers will be bright."

"But pink matches your personality." Andrea brought forward the blouses she'd picked out. Carly did like them, especially the white top with cherry blossoms. She took the shirts from Andrea and slipped into the dressing room.

She put on the cherry blossom blouse first and whipped the curtain open. "What do you think, Andrea?"

"It's Andy." The woman smiled. "I've told you a dozen times. *Andy.*"

Carly grinned back. "What do you think, Andy?" She'd worn a denim skirt for shopping, hoping to find the perfect accent to the flirty, knee-length piece.

"It's adorable," Andy said.

Carly frowned, and Andy's eyes widened. "Oh, it seems we're not going for adorable. It's flirty. Fun. Sexy."

Carly threw her head back and laughed. She wore a white

camisole under the flimsy fabric of the cherry blossom shirt. It was fun and flirty. But it wasn't sexy. Maybe just the right amount of cute combined with sophisticated.

"Does it say, *Hey, I'm ready for you to kiss me*?" Carly turned to check how the fabric hung down the back.

"Ooh, are you going to the Tulip Festival with someone special?"

Carly couldn't help the insta-smile that popped onto her face. "Just this guy I met at work."

"This is the perfect thing. And you can wear it out."

Wear it out, Carly did. After paying, she headed home where she should've unpacked a box, but instead she sat in the recliner in her bedroom and read a novel she'd read a dozen times before.

REESE HADN'T FELT LIKE HE NEEDED AN ANTI-ANXIETY PILL FOR years. Even the recent injury hadn't prompted him to start popping the anti-depressants Carly had brought home from the hospital. But as he pulled into Carly's driveway, his heart raced, and his palms turned slick with sweat, and his vocal chords seized.

It felt like a panic attack, and with the still-injured status of his ribs, he couldn't get a decent breath. The episode passed quickly, but left Reese out of sorts. He could barely get himself out of the truck, and walking up her sidewalk to the front door seemed like it took hours.

She flounced out the front door before he'd climbed a single step, and the sight of her brought a calm balm to Reese's quaking soul.

"Hey, Sergeant." She skipped down the steps in her denim skirt and a gauzy top with bright pink cherry blossoms on it. She wore stylish shoes, the kind that laced up to the ankle.

Reese whistled. "Well, don't you look mighty fine?" He swept his arm around her waist and pulled her close, the earlier worry completely gone now that they were together. "You ready to see some tulips?"

She giggled as he swung her around, both her hands coming up to grip his left shoulder. "You don't look so bad yourself." She fiddled with a button on his polo, and her fingers flirted with his before settling into place.

He'd chosen his clothes carefully, but didn't have much selection. Jeans, T-shirts, long-sleeved plaid shirts, cowboy boots, cowboy hat. With the near-summer weather, he'd gone with a polo in tangerine, the website had called it.

"Do you wear pink, too?" she teased as they moved back to his truck.

"As a matter of fact, I have a blue and pink plaid shirt. I'll wear it on Monday."

Her blonde curls danced along his forearm as she tipped her head back and laughed. "Can't wait to see it." She boosted herself up into the truck, and Reese went around the back to get to the driver's seat.

When he opened his door, she'd scooted across the bench seat, barely leaving him enough room to get in and put both hands on the steering wheel. The air between them felt charged, electric, as he drove to the botanical gardens on the south end of town.

The conversation came easy. Her fingers in his felt natural. He used his military ID to purchase discount admission tickets and lemonades, and they set off on the self-guided tour of all things tulip. Families and couples, senior citizen groups and friends, thronged the wide walkways.

A sinking feeling had Reese tightening his grip on Carly's hand as they maneuvered through the people to see the heirloom purple and yellow tulips that had been planted to display the letters LSU.

"Probably shouldn't have come on opening weekend," he

grumbled. He'd hoped for more privacy, for an opportunity to kiss Carly with the heady scent of flowers in the air.

"It's fine," she said. "We're not in a hurry."

She was right, and Reese slowed his pace. He hadn't brought his wheelchair, determined not to let her push him around on their date. He had noticed that he could rent a golf cart, and as the afternoon wore on and they still hadn't seen all two-hundred-fifty-thousand tulips, that possibility grew ever nearer.

The crowd thinned as evening fell, as everyone went to dinner, and back to grandparent's houses for ice cream.

"Should we go?" Carly asked, peering at the map. "Or should we try to see the *tulipa acuminata*? They're these yellow and red tulips called Fire Flames, and the petals on top are long, like flames. Look." She pushed the brochure at him, and he glanced at the unusual tulips.

"We could go after we see these," she said. "I'm starving."

"Sure," he said. "Let's see those, and then we'll go."

She bounced ahead of him, and he marveled at her energy. Their lemonade had run out long ago, as had his patience. But Carly babbled about flowers like she had a personal investment in them. Her infectious optimism had him admiring bed after bed of tulips as he listened to her read about them from the brochure.

She'd claimed to dislike small towns, but as far as Reese could tell, she'd assimilated in no time at all. She had men asking her out, no problem finding anything—despite her claims—and didn't seem to dislike Three Rivers at all. Incredible hope soared through him. Maybe she could be happy here. Maybe she could be happy here with him.

She waited for him at a corner, and he noticed that the crowd back this far was non-existent. She looped her arm through his and they continued under the canopy of shade toward a tulip display at the end of the sidewalk. A couple turned from their admiration of the flowers and headed toward Reese and Carly.

Once they left, Reese would be alone with Carly. Finally alone.

His heart galloped like a herd of wild horses, and he wondered if Jim, the horseman on *The Man From Snowy River*, had felt like this just before kissing Jessica.

He stumbled, and Carly's grip on his arm tightened. She read from the brochure. Grinned at the flowers.

Reese couldn't think about anything besides what it might feel like to kiss her.

"Reese?" she asked.

"Hmm?" How could he do it? Should he just grab her and kiss her? It had been so, so long since he'd felt anything for a woman, and even longer since he'd kissed one. Since he'd even *thought* about kissing one.

"Have you heard anything I've said?"

He glanced at her, and the blush in her face drove his desire through the roof. "Yeah, 'course. *Tulipa*...something. Fire Flame." He gestured toward the grand display of fiery flowers.

She caught his hand as it fell to his side. "Not that. I asked you a question."

She pressed in closer to him, and his mouth went dry. "You did?"

"I knew you weren't listening." She smiled, and Reese took her in his arms. It felt so good, so right, to hold her close, sway with her, listen to the sound of her breathing and feel her pulse against his.

"Carly, I don't know what you said, and I'm real sorry about that. But can it wait one more minute?"

"I guess—"

"Because I might combust if I can't kiss you right now." He ducked his head lower, his lips skating along the top of her ear toward her cheek. "Can I kiss you, beautiful?"

"See, now, *I'm* listening, so I can answer that question. And if *you'd* been listening, you'd know that I asked you how many more dates you were going to take me on without kissing me."

Reese pulled back the tiniest bit, far enough to look into her eyes. He found a sparkle of laughter and joy, but she wasn't joking. She really had asked him that, and he'd missed it.

"None." He leaned down and pressed his lips to hers, excited when she received his mouth with eagerness. Everything around him fell into silence. He couldn't even smell the exotic flowers anymore, because his whole world was consumed with kissing Carly.

## 11

Carly's euphoria didn't start to fade until Reese pulled into her driveway. He killed the engine and cut the lights, and she realized the most perfect, beautiful day was ending.

"Thank you for dinner," she said. He'd taken her somewhere quiet, in a town about thirty minutes west of Three Rivers. "I've never had Indian food before. It was good."

"I'm glad you liked the curry." His strong voice barely reached her ears. They'd driven to Pampa in near silence, the low warbling of country music a background so Carly could re-live the best kiss of her life over and over and over. And over.

"Well, I guess I better go in." She turned toward him, glad when he lifted his arm over her shoulder and drew her in for another kiss. She felt very much like a schoolgirl, kissing her boyfriend for as long as possible before her father flashed the porch light and she had to go in.

She enjoyed the kiss, the warmth of Reese's arms, for one last moment before pulling away. "Best date ever," she whispered at the same time she scooted toward the passenger door. "See you at church tomorrow?"

He nodded and she got out of the truck. She moved up the sidewalk to the porch, where she turned back and waved to Reese. She couldn't quite see his face because of the shadows and his cowboy hat, but he looked a little stormy.

She ducked inside and texted him. *Are you okay?*

*Fine.*

*What's wrong?* She moved away from the front door, though she hadn't heard his truck start.

*Mad I couldn't walk you to the door. Okay?*

She started to respond, but didn't finish before he sent another message. *I'm fine. See you tomorrow.*

Carly pressed her phone over her pulse. Reese was a proud man, a valiant soldier. Of course he'd be upset he was so tired he couldn't walk her to the door. But at least she'd gotten her kiss.

She grinned as she readied herself for bed, grateful for such a beautiful day, this beautiful town, and that beautiful man.

---

CARLY WAITED IN THE LOBBY AT CHURCH, FIXING THE NECKLACE against her chest, fiddling with the bangles on her wrist, tugging at the hem of her skirt. Reese should've arrived five minutes ago, and she'd never known the man to be late.

Worry needled her mind. She'd woken with thoughts of Lindsay in her head. She needed to call and confess everything. Confess her feelings. Confess the kiss. Fear had kept her silent, along with her reasoning that her relationship with Reese hadn't affected her job performance.

Still, guilt gripped her heart, and it struggled to beat against the phone call she should make.

And Reese wasn't here. Had something happened to him? Another fall? Too exhausted after all that walking yesterday afternoon? She'd seen him fading after only an hour, but she hadn't been able to suggest leaving. She'd wanted to kiss him at the botanical gardens so badly, she just couldn't.

Organ music leaked from the chapel, and Carly took one last peek out the door and into the parking lot. Reese limped toward her as fast as she'd ever seen him. She waved, but he didn't see her, singular in his task to get to the doors.

He noticed her when he only had a few steps remaining, and a grin graced his gorgeous face. "Mornin'."

"I was starting to worry about you."

"Well, ain't that a nice thing to hear?" He tucked her into his side as he continued into the chapel. "Haven't had anyone worryin' about me in a while." With his late arrival, the only seats left were on the left side, near the middle.

Reese didn't seem fazed as he shuffled forward and slid onto the pew. Carly felt the weight of every eye as she sat and he lifted his arm over her shoulder. Engulfed in the warmth of his skin, and the scent of his aftershave, she decided she didn't care what the townspeople thought of her.

Her boss, on the other hand, Carly wondered what she would think of the relationship.

As the pastor spoke about faith and taking steps that seemed scary, a feeling of contentment washed over Carly. She'd done that—had faith and taken steps into the unknown—when she moved to Three Rivers. When she'd allowed herself to open up to Reese. When she'd kissed him.

*Hold on a little longer*, she thought as the choir stood to sing. If the grants came through, she could leave her job at the public clinic. She had a Master's degree in social work. She was a licensed, nonclinical social worker who'd completed her supervision hours and passed her jurisprudence exam. Her license didn't expire for another year—she had time to get things figured out.

REESE STEPPED NEXT TO PETE AND CHELSEA ON THE FRINGE OF THE picnic. Pete carried his daughter on his shoulders, and she babbled in baby tongues as more people streamed over to the park from the church.

"How was the Tulip Festival?" Chelsea asked Carly, and every muscle in Reese's body turned to stone.

"So beautiful," Carly gushed. "I had no idea there were so many kinds of tulips."

"Which one was your favorite?"

She shot a glance at Reese that sent fire down to the tips of his cowboy boots. "The Fire Flame. Very explosive."

"That your favorite too, Sergeant?" Pete asked, his watchful eye zeroed in on Reese.

Reese cleared his throat. "I liked the blueberries and cream."

"Those were the first ones we saw," Carly said, the enthusiasm in her voice turning down a decibel.

"And after that, they sort of blurred together," he added.

Pete chuckled and Chelsea playfully slapped Reese's arm. "Well, it sounds like you were a good sport at least."

Carly's wounded look didn't escape him, and Reese lifted his eyebrows in a silent question: *What?*

She drew him away from his friends with a pout and a quick nod of her head. "You didn't like the Tulip Festival?"

"I liked it fine."

"Did the flowers really all blur together?"

Reese didn't quite know what she wanted him to say. "All except that last one."

That coaxed a smile from her. "I thought you were having a good time. Before that, I mean."

"I was." He snaked his arm around her waist. "I was with you. I had a great time."

She narrowed her eyes at him. "You get a pass this time, Sergeant. Next time, though, we do something we both like." She turned to join the mass of people lining up for food.

"Carly, I liked it fine."

She spun back to him. "If you say *fine* one more time, I can't predict what I'll do." She pressed her palm into his and practically dragged him into line.

"Are you really mad?" he whispered as the line inched forward.

"A little," she admitted. "I really thought yesterday was the greatest day of my life, and now I find out that you were suffering." She scanned him from head to toe. "Physically and mentally." She picked up a plate and handed it to him. "Why didn't you say something?"

He focused on adding potato salad to his plate. "You seemed to really enjoy it. Didn't want to ruin it."

She slapped a spoonful of baked beans on her plate, practically splattering them everywhere. "Well, this is ruining it."

"Only if you let it." He picked up a wheat roll and knifed butter on top.

She didn't answer, and he glanced up to find her staring at him. "You're right."

"Okay." Reese blinked at her, unsure of what else to say.

"I had a great time yesterday."

"So did I."

"Okay." She tucked her hair behind her ear and moved down the line. Reese watched her, a keen sense of admiration threading through him.

"Watch it, Sergeant," Squire said, sidling up beside Reese and taking a scoop of frog eye salad. "I've seen that look on a man's face before, and I'd say you're fallin' hard."

Reese ducked his head so his cowboy hat bathed his face in shadows.

"She *is* pretty," Squire said. "You kiss her at the Tulip Festival?"

"Do *not* answer that," Kelly said, hipping Squire back a step. "Honorable men don't kiss and tell."

Reese pressed his lips together, determined to be the honorable man Carly deserved.

---

"CARLY IS A LICENSED, NONCLINICAL SOCIAL WORKER," REESE argued. Pete sat as still as a statue, his arms folded across his chest. He hadn't moved in five minutes. "She deserves a salary to reflect that."

"PATH won't approve it," Pete said. "And we need them to approve this grant."

Reese wanted to stab the pen through the table. "There are a dozen facilities across the country that have on-site social workers for their clients. They fill out government forms, research programs for the veterans, ensure they're getting their proper medical care. Carly would be ten times busier than she is now, and it would be a real draw for Courage Reins over the Heart Warriors Center in Amarillo."

Reese pushed the pen closer to Pete. "And if PATH doesn't approve her position, we can put it on another grant. The equine therapy one, maybe. They like innovative and interesting proposals."

Pete looked over his shoulder as someone entered the building. "Gwen's here. I need to talk to her."

"Please, Lieutenant. Just sign the form." Reese picked up the pen and held it out for Pete to take.

He stood. "You sure this isn't just about you and her?"

"If we don't get this grant, there is no me and her." He sighed, but it sounded more like a growl. "So yeah, some of this is about me and her."

Pete's stony façade cracked, and a low chuckle escaped his lips. "Well, at least you're honest." He pushed open the door of the conference room. "Gwen, in here."

The tall, dark-haired woman twisted at the sound of his voice and her face broke into a smile as she entered the conference room.

"You aren't using your cane," Pete said.

"The doctor says the cancer is gone." Her smile could've lit the darkest night.

"I was just goin' to ask about your appointment." Pete embraced her. "That's such great news."

"You don't have a riding lesson today," Reese said, thumbing through the calendar on his phone. "What brings you all the way out to Three Rivers?"

"You," she said, grinning. "I wanted to thank you personally for helping me with the insurance paperwork for the bone marrow transplant. Without you...." She shook her head, emotion rendering her unable to continue. She shoved a paper bag toward him.

Reese waved his hand like his help meant nothing, but he'd researched for days to find what Gwen had needed to get the funding for her transplant. And the codes he'd needed for every ticky-tacky little hospital abbreviation? A nightmare.

"Take it," Gwen insisted. "I'm not the greatest cook, but I've been taking lessons from Heidi Ackerman."

Reese's eyebrows rose. "Doesn't Chelsea take those too?" He glanced at Pete.

"Every week, and I'm not complaining." He leaned down and sniffed the bag. "I'll take it if you don't want it, Sergeant. Smells like cinnamon rolls."

Reese snatched the bag before Pete could rob him of his treat. "I earned this by searching for government health codes for days. Stand down, Lieutenant."

"I remember that," Pete said, glancing at Reese. "You worked hard on that."

"We're trying to get a licensed social worker," Reese said, piercing Pete with a pointed glare. "So we can keep helping our clients with things like this." He gave Gwen a quick side-hug. "Come on. Maybe Miss Kelly has lunch at the homestead."

"She does." Pete bent, picked up the pen, and signed the PATH International grant renewal form—with Carly's proposed social worker position. "It's tacos today."

WEEKS PASSED, AND REESE'S HANDS TREMBLED EVERY AFTERNOON as he collected the mail and took it inside to his desk to open. PATH International usually sent acceptances out before rejections, and finally, Reese saw the envelope he'd been waiting for.

He clutched the letter-size packet in his fist and closed his eyes. Though the letter was already printed, sealed, mailed, and he couldn't change it, Reese prayed anyway. *Please, God.* His daily ministrations had been more eloquent, but as his heart tore through his chest like a wild bull, he couldn't come up with anything more.

He ripped open the envelope and pulled out the sheaf of papers. The top page said *Congratulations!* and he knew they'd gotten the grant. He hadn't doubted they would. What was in question was the amount, and how it was to be allocated. He had to keep a tight ship, reporting every penny spent at the non-profit, and Reese liked making the numbers line up.

Flipping the page, he found the overall budget. It was identical to last year's.

No clinical social worker.

His heart tumbled to his boots, especially when Carly's fingers squeezed his shoulder. "That the mail?"

He couldn't look at her. "Yeah." He handed her the budget sheet, his vocal chords tight tight tight.

A few seconds of silence passed while she studied it. While Reese waited for her to exhale and make a proclamation that she had to move back to Amarillo.

The sigh came, and it sounded so defeated. "We didn't get it."

He shook his head, wishing he could create a different reality for her. "I'll put it on the equine therapy grant. Theirs is forty percent of our funding."

"Reese—"

"Don't tell me not to." He glanced up at her, fire boiling through his blood. "We still have a chance for this."

She pulled over a chair and sat next to him. "You said PATH was our best chance."

He had said that, because it was true. "Doesn't mean it's our only chance."

She looked over the counter, out the front door of the building, her gaze on something far away. Something only she could see. "I need to call my boss."

Reese pulled open a filing drawer and took out the already completed application for the equine therapy program. "I just need Pete to sign this." He stood, the ache in his hip radiating up and infecting the fleshy parts of his heart. "Then I'll get it mailed off. It should only take a couple of weeks to hear back." He leaned down and pressed a kiss to her temple. "Wait until we hear back from them, okay?"

She tilted her head back to look at him, and he kissed her, hoping to infuse her with all the emotions thundering through him. He pulled back before he would've liked, and asked, "Can you just wait a couple more weeks before you call your boss?"

She nodded, and he made a hasty exit before she changed her mind.

## 12

Carly puttered around her kitchen, putting together a solitary meal of spaghetti and meatballs. She went through the motions of putting water on to boil, of browning ground beef, of opening a can of sauce and setting a timer on the angel hair pasta.

She didn't have to think about cooking, keeping her mind free to roam around the possibilities for a future at Courage Reins.

No matter how many times she tried to come up with a solution, she always ended up in the same place: Unemployed and back in Amarillo.

Her only hope was the equine therapy grant, and that was no guarantee.

*Call Lindsay,* she thought as she drained the noodles and added them to the waiting meat sauce.

But Reese had begged her to wait for the grant to come back. She'd said she would. Still, something nagged at her stomach, and it wasn't hunger though she hadn't eaten since breakfast. She forced her dinner down a too-narrow throat and settled in front of the TV with her laptop in position.

She needed to find another job. One that paid well enough to keep her house in Three Rivers, pay off her student loans, and keep her in her car and current lifestyle. She searched for doctor's offices, hospitals, schools, and anywhere else where someone might employ a social worker.

She made a list, but with only one elementary school, one middle school, and one high school, the prospects in education seemed limited. Three Rivers housed one hospital, one insta-care, and a half-dozen doctors offices. An academy for children with mental disabilities lay on the outskirts of town, and Carly circled the name of it. That was her best chance.

Satisfied that she was doing something productive, she closed her laptop and turned her attention to the reality program on the TV. But she didn't watch. Her mind turned circles around the list she'd made, wondering how long it would take to get a new job. Wondering if Reese was worth the effort.

The following morning, she texted Reese that she had a couple of errands to run before she came out to the ranch. She stopped by two doctors offices—one a general family practice, and one a pediatric practice—before heading out to Mill Creek Academy.

The general family practice needed someone part-time to call insurance companies and validate paperwork. The job sounded less than ideal to Carly, especially for someone with her credentials, but something had to be done. She couldn't keep living with the guilt.

The secretary at Mill Creek buzzed her into the office, and she hitched on her best smile. "Hello. I'm wondering if I can speak with Mister Hillman." She'd done her homework on the academy.

"He's down in the cafeteria." The secretary glanced at her computer screen for a second. "He'll be back in about ten minutes. Can you wait?"

"Sure." Carly seated herself on the couch, her insides already knotting. By the time she'd seen three parents come in with their mentally disabled children, Carly wondered what she was doing. She hadn't specialized in mental illnesses. She wasn't a clinical social worker. Her confidence fell further when a giant of a man came through the door.

"Bev, have you seen Miss Harvey this morning?" His booming voice left little doubt as to who ran this place.

"Yes, she just checked in her son not five minutes ago. Did you need her?"

Mr. Hillman smiled. "Nope. Just makin' sure Julian got here today."

Bev, the secretary, nodded toward Carly. "This woman would like to speak with you."

He turned toward her, and Carly stood, her heels barely supporting her weight. "Sure. Come on in." He smiled and waved her into his office, where he closed the door and settled behind his huge desk. "What can I help you with?"

"I'm a licensed, nonclinical social worker. I'm wondering if you need anything like that here at Mill Creek."

He regarded her for a moment past comfortable. "We have a psychologist on-staff," he said. "And a speech pathologist, and a nurse. Together, they handle most of our social work needs."

Carly's throat felt like someone had tarred and feathered it. She opened her mouth to speak, but no noise came out.

"I have a friend in Oklahoma City," he said, reaching for a pad of sticky notes on his desk. "I think he said he was looking for someone like you to start up next school year." He scribbled something on the paper. "Here's his name and number. Maybe you can give him a call."

Carly took the sticky note, which somehow unstuck her vocal chords. "Thank you, Mister Hillman."

"I don't know what he's looking for, exactly. And maybe he's already found someone."

"I'll call." Carly stood and extended her hand for him to

shake. He stood too, and she felt a sense of happiness wash through her. "Thank you for your kindness."

"Good luck."

She ducked out of his office. In the safety of her little car, she dialed the number on the sticky note, sending a prayer heavenward as the line rang.

---

CARLY DIDN'T TELL REESE ABOUT THE VISIT TO THE ACADEMY. OR the hospital. Or the insta-care. She turned in applications at the doctor's offices, but no one called. She didn't want to burden him, didn't want to add to the balloon of hope he carried that she'd be able to stay on at Courage Reins.

She had an interview in Oklahoma City the second week of July, but she didn't tell Reese about that either. The director of the school there, Doctor Yancey, had said he wasn't really looking for a social worker, but a suitable psychologist hadn't applied either. She'd wanted to come right away, but he needed to finish the school year, and then he was going on vacation, and the second week of July was the soonest he could meet with her.

She sat at her desk in her microscopic office at Courage Reins, pushing paper around. With only three veterans, she didn't have a whole lot to do. At least Stephen was coming out for his lesson that afternoon.

"Carly." Reese's call from the front desk made her heartbeat skip. "Come here, would you?"

She joined him in the reception area, and he had an envelope cinched in his fist. "The equine therapy grant."

She couldn't breathe. Her heart banged against her ribcage, and she couldn't quiet it. She'd given up on praying to get her salary approved by the grant. She didn't feel quite right about it, and she hadn't been able to keep asking God for something if she wasn't supposed to get it.

Not that getting the grant was wrong. But continuing a relationship with Reese without telling her boss—that was.

Reese tore into the envelope, and the look of hope in his eyes dimmed with each sentence he read. Carly didn't need to take the piece of paper he lifted toward her to know her salary hadn't been approved.

"We still have—"

"No." She shook her head. "Reese, it's not going to work out." Bricks settled in her gut as she spoke, but her voice sounded strong. She knew she'd spoken the truth, harsh and hard to hear as it was.

He usually wouldn't look at her when he existed in turmoil. But now, he did. Everything he felt about her sat right on his face. She heard the adoration and desperation he carried when he said, "What are you going to do?"

"Call my boss." She straightened her skirt. "It's the right thing to do. I should've done it weeks ago."

"But—"

"I'll likely get put on probation," she said, vocalizing what they'd never talked about. "I'll get paid for a month or two, maybe. But I'll lose my job." She didn't look away from him as she moved closer and crouched in front of him. She took both of his hands in hers. "I'll find another job."

"Doing what?"

"I've been applying at the hospital, the doctor's offices." Her voice caught on telling him about the school in Oklahoma City. But she dug down deep to her well of courage. "I've got an interview at a special-needs school in Oklahoma City in a couple of weeks."

"Oklahoma City?" His voice sounded like he'd swallowed glass. "That's—"

"About three and a half hours," she said. "I can come visit on the weekends."

His face fell and his ducked his head so his cowboy hat hid

his eyes. Classic Reese. "I don't want a visitor on the weekends. There's another grant I can try to put your salary on."

"No," she said again, this time with more gentleness in her tone. "I can't keep begging the Lord for a blessing when I'm not being honest." She started to remove her hands from his, but he gripped them tighter. "I can't, Reese."

He nodded, made eye contact, and tried on a smile. It made his already handsome face beautiful, but it didn't quite light up his eyes the way it usually did. "What do you need me to do?"

"Nothing." She freed her hands from his, took his hat in her right hand, and cradled his cheek in her left. Her eyes drifted closed as she inched closer to him, and when his lips met hers, she hoped this wasn't the last time she kissed him.

---

CARLY RETREATED TO HER OFFICE AND CLOSED THE DOOR. REESE let her go, though he wanted to be in the room with her when she called her boss. It didn't seem fair, and resentment welled in his core, pressed against his lungs, reminded him of how easily everything came to those around him. All six of his older brothers. The other men in his unit. Everyone but him.

The one person he'd felt a connection to in years, and he couldn't have her without causing a big problem for her.

No, the situation was all kinds of unfair.

A door behind him closed and footsteps came down the hall. Reese recognized them as Pete's, and he got up from the desk. He hurried toward the restroom, because he didn't want to look into his friend's face. Didn't want to tell Pete that he'd been right. Didn't want to explain about Carly already looking for other jobs, about Carly calling her boss, about how he'd failed Carly.

He stayed in the bathroom until he felt sure Pete had left. Sure enough, when he came out, the reception area sat empty, the air conditioning buzzing through the vents the only sound. Carly's door was still closed. He'd barely taken his position behind the counter when Pete popped his head out of the conference room.

"There you are. Can you come in here?"

Reese heaved himself back to standing. "Sure, boss." He expected to find a new client waiting with Pete—that was the only time Reese got called into the conference room with the owner of Courage Reins.

But only Pete sat at the table. No new file. No client. Nothing.

Pete closed the door, and Reese felt trapped. Trapped behind brick and glass. Trapped beneath metal, as it dug into his hip, and smoke burned his eyes, and his bones cracked and splintered and his future died.

"I just saw Carly get in her car and leave," Pete said, leveling a serious look at Reese. "She was cryin'."

Reese felt like crying too, but he shoved the emotion down inside himself where Pete couldn't see it. A muscle in his jaw twitched as he clenched his teeth.

"Somethin' happen with you two?"

Reese shook his head. Nothing had happened, and that was the problem. She wasn't even coming over in the evenings anymore. For the past couple of weeks, he'd been driving himself to work as she "ran errands" that he now knew to be her job hunting.

"I saw the grant came through from the equine therapy corporation."

Then he knew why she'd left crying. Slivers of Reese's heart flaked off as he thought about her driving in her purple car, distraught. He wondered if he'd see her again, if he could call her and ask her to come to dinner with him.

"Yeah," Reese ground out past the anger in his soul. "Everything seems to be on course for Courage Reins."

"But not for Carly to be our social worker."

Reese wanted to throw his hands into the air and ask Pete what to do. "Remember when you were livin' in that tent? While your house wasn't quite built yet?" he asked. "This is like that. Carly leaving...I'm the one in the tent, Lieutenant, and no one can convince me that it's better somewhere else."

Pete's chin dropped to his chest as understanding bloomed in his eyes. "What's she gonna do?"

"My guess is she just got placed on probation," Reese said. "And that she'll lose her job with the clinic in Amarillo. She's been lookin' for another job." He cleared the catch in his throat. "But there's not much in Three Rivers for a woman like Carly."

"You're in Three Rivers."

Reese stood, his frustration and fear and fury reaching a boiling point. "Like I said, not much here for someone like her."

---

REESE DIDN'T CALL HER THAT EVENING, THOUGH HE CLENCHED HIS phone in his hand until his bones ached. They didn't ride to work together—Carly didn't come to Courage Reins at all. Weak as he was, Reese texted her about mid-morning.

*You're not coming in?*

*Can't*, was all she said.

*I miss you.*

*I'm driving to Oklahoma City right now. I'll call you tonight.*

Reese left work early, something he almost never did, because he didn't have anything worth rushing home for. But that day, he couldn't stand being at Courage Reins, seeing the progress their clients made, when he felt like his life had taken a dozen steps backward. He picked up a loaf of bread at the grocery store and made toast and eggs for dinner, his phone turned all the way up and never more than six inches from his hand.

Carly took her sweet time calling, and by the time his phone rang, Reese's nerves felt like they'd been sliced into ribbons.

"Hey, Sergeant," she said when he answered.

His ragged edges smoothed with the sound of her voice. "Hey, yourself," he said. "How's Oklahoma City?"

"It's much bigger than Amarillo." Reese heard the frown in her voice. "Noisier." She sighed. "But there are a lot of job opportunities here."

A stab of disquiet kept Reese from answering. He did not want Carly to move to Oklahoma City, but everything he'd thought of to keep her in Three Rivers had failed. Short of buying a diamond ring....

He seized onto the idea, but almost instantly let it go. She'd say no. He didn't love her anyway. Not yet, though he certainly felt like he'd taken the first steps toward falling in love with her. She was the first woman who'd so much as attracted his attention in so long that he wanted to step carefully, not leap when he should tiptoe.

"Will you be back for the Fourth of July?" Reese asked. "Some friends of mine are comin' into town, and the Ackerman's are having a big party for Finn...." Reese didn't want to go alone. He thought sitting in his house with all the curtains closed would be better than trailing along with all the couples.

"Who's coming into town?"

"A friend who lived at the ranch a couple of summers ago. Brett Murphy, and his wife, Kate. They live in North Carolina, but always come to Three Rivers for the Fourth." Reese had attended Finn's birthday party for years, and he appreciated the example of family and faith Squire and Kelly, and Pete and Chelsea, and Brett and Kate, had provided. He'd never felt out of place among them, though he was unattached. He'd always been okay with it.

This year, though, he thought it might just be the worst form of torture to attend the birthday party without Carly. He didn't begrudge his friends for their happiness. He just wanted it for himself too. He'd never really known what he was missing—until Carly came driving into town—and right into his life—in that purple car.

He asked her about the hospitals where she'd submitted her application, and she outlined her plans for the next day.

"What did your boss say?" he finally got the courage to ask.

"She put me on administrative probation pending an investigation." She coughed, and scuffling came through the line while she took a drink. "She'll probably come out there and talk to you tomorrow."

He didn't want to talk to anyone about Carly.

"Her name's Lindsay, just so you know. She said she'd call."

"Maybe I can save her the drive, then." Reese hated that his voice sounded like someone else's. That he'd have to talk about his relationship with Carly—which felt so right and so perfect to him—like it was dishonest or scandalous.

"After that, I'm sure she'll find I violated the protocols for the clinic, and I'll lose my job. But yes, I should be home for the Fourth of July. My interview at the special-needs school is the following week, but I can't afford to stay in a hotel for two weeks."

Reese wished he had the financial means to take care of her, but the cold fact was, he didn't. The grant from Courage Reins paid him a fair salary, but it wasn't enough to take over her bills too.

"When will you be home?" he asked. "Because I miss you like crazy." He couldn't imagine her being gone all week, only to see her on weekends, if then.

"I'll be back in time for church on Sunday."

Four days. Reese had to endure the next four days on his own. He didn't know how he'd done it before she came into his life, because the idea of weathering ninety-six hours by himself put him in a foul mood that he couldn't shake away.

"Church on Sunday sounds great," he said, making his tone as cheerful as possible. Which meant it sounded like a growl instead of a hiss. He said good-bye, avoided a call from his father by silencing his phone, and wandered into the backyard to contemplate the summer night sky.

---

THE HOURS SPENT BEHIND THE DESK AT COURAGE REINS turned into captors, and Reese could only stay contained by the walls of the building for a few hours before restlessness took him out to the barn.

He visited with Elvis, and exercised Peony since she had no clients for the rest of the week, and even ventured over to the ranch horses to brush down Arrowhead after he'd spent the day moving a large section of the herd from one field to another.

His time with the horses soothed him as much as it reminded him that his best friends had four legs and hooves. When the ache for Carly pressed beneath his breastbone, he returned to Courage Reins.

Pete caught him before he could enter the building. "Havin' a barbeque at our place on Friday night. You're welcome to come."

Reese seized onto the invitation, hardly letting himself think through an evening with two families—and him, solo. Reese loved kids. He felt like he could relate to them in ways he couldn't with adults.

He wanted kids of his own, but he'd given up the hope somewhere between Germany and the United States. Of course, he'd abandoned the idea of ever finding someone who could see the man behind the limp too, and Carly seemed to be able to do that.

"Reese?" Pete peered at him. "You want to come?"

"Yeah." Reese grinned at the lieutenant. "I want to come."

Pete returned the smile. "Great. Bring some of your famous baked beans." He clapped Reese on the shoulder and continued on his way. Reese watched him go, his scarred hand swinging at his side.

Hope coiled through Reese with the force of a tight spring. Pete had found someone to see past his deformities. He and Chelsea had made it work. Reese could only hope—and pray— that he and Carly could too.

———

SUNDAY CAME, AS SUNDAYS ALWAYS DID, AND ANTICIPATION hummed in Reese's veins. He arrived at church earlier than usual and took a seat in the back row. He didn't normally sit so far away, but something inside him wanted to blend into the crowd today.

Soon enough, the chapel filled and the organ began playing. When Pastor Scott stood up and Carly still hadn't come in, disappointment swept through Reese. He tried to focus on the pastor's words, but they blurred into highs and lows of sound.

As soon as the service ended, he stood and hobbled into the lobby. He needed to get home before anyone saw him slinking away by himself. He heard someone call his name, but he pretended like he didn't.

Soon enough, though, Pete caught up to him. "Where you goin' so fast? It's like the devil himself is after you."

"I just need to get home."

"You aren't comin' to the best picnic of the summer?"

Reese stalled. Dave Rimms owned a barbeque Dutch oven catering company, and he brought his signature baby back pork ribs to exactly one picnic: the one before the Fourth of July. Reese's mouth watered just thinking about the ribs—and Dave's Dutch oven potatoes.

"Besides," Pete said, twisting back the way he'd come. "Carly's been frantic to find you since she slid onto the bench next to Chelsea."

Reese looked over Pete's shoulder and saw a blonde woman walking toward them, with Chelsea beside her, holding a toddler's hand as she navigated the dirt parking lot.

Everything tight inside him released. "Carly's here."

"Brett got in last night too." Pete smiled at the group moving toward them. "Kate's been dyin' to see you."

Sure enough, the fiery red-head quickened her step when she saw Reese standing next to Pete. "Reese Sanders." She swept her eyes up and down him. "It's so good to see you." She engulfed him in a hug, though she was half his size. He felt her love and concern all the way down to his toes, and gratitude filled him from top to bottom.

"Hey, Kate."

She stepped back and nudged her son forward. "Go on now. You remember Reese."

"Hello, Sergeant Sanders." Reid held out his hand for Reese to shake. He swept the boy into his arms and swung him around with a chuckle from him and a gleeful laugh from the boy.

Brett grinned as Reese set Reid on the ground. "You haven't met Maddy yet."

The little girl stared at Reese with wide eyes. Her strawberry blonde hair suggested she'd look more like Kate than Brett, who wore a full beard of dark hair and sported eyes the color of coal.

"It's good to see you," Reese said through a throat thick with emotion. Brett clapped him on the back and stepped to the side so Reese could get a full view of Carly. She hung back, out of the way, but she was like a drink of fresh water after a long time on the range.

"Birthday party tomorrow for Finn at six," Kelly announced, joining the group. "What are we standin' here for?" She fanned herself. "It's hot. Let's get to the park."

The group moved off, leaving Reese with Carly in the sweltering, dirt parking lot. The July heat waves practically blurred her perfect image.

"Hey," she said.

"I didn't see you come in," he said. "I was sittin' in the back so

I could see you come in." Truth was, after the meeting started, he'd stopped looking. He'd sort of turned numb.

"I was a little late. I couldn't find you, so I just sat by Pete and Chelsea."

He moved forward and gathered her into his arms. "I missed you so much." He breathed in the strawberry scent of her hair, ran his hands down the curve of her back. He tilted her back and kissed her, right there in the parking lot.

And she kissed him back, right there in the parking lot.

## 13

Carly sat on the bench at a large picnic table in a beautiful, Texas backyard. Kelly Ackerman bustled around, adjusting the birthday presents and stopping by the grill where her dad stood. She kissed him on the cheek and gave her mom a quick hug before calling the partygoers together.

Carly didn't know everyone really well, but with Reese at her side, she didn't need to. They loved and accepted him, and by association, her. Chelsea chatted with her easily, asked her about Oklahoma City and her family and her job prospects. Kate wasn't as chatty, but she radiated warmth and offered her friendship without qualification.

"Finn," Kelly called. "Squire! Time to eat." She turned back to her mom and muttered something about how her husband and son could get carried away when it came to football.

Carly watched the pair with fondness, wondering if Reese would be able to play with his kids the same way. His grip on her shoulder tightened as if he could read her thoughts. His physical injuries probably wouldn't allow him to run and play as much as

Squire and Finn did, though Squire's limp certainly hindered him some.

The party proceeded, with conversation about the ranch and the horses. Brett kept his questions coming, and Carly suspected he didn't want to answer any about his own life. Soon enough, though, Pete asked about the estate in North Carolina. Kate answered most of the questions while Brett kept his mouth full.

"Best part is, Brett's retiring from the Army next month." She tucked her arm in his.

Squire and Pete exchanged a glance. "That's great news, Brett. What are you gonna do next?"

"I just licensed my construction firm," he said. "I'm opening the doors in two weeks."

"But he's already got more work than he can handle." Kate beamed at him. "And he's teaching riding lessons on the estate on the weekends. His kids' camp starts next weekend."

Brett ducked his head at his wife's obvious adoration.

"Kids' camp?" Pete asked. He nodded at Reese. "That's a great idea." He swung back to Squire. "You could help with that, Major."

"Set it up," Squire said. "Reese can get people out to the ranch. Everyone loves 'im."

A flash of pride stole through her. Everyone did love Reese. When she'd called the pastor to set up meals for him, the assignments had filled in less than ten minutes.

"I don't know any kids," Reese said.

"But you know their moms and dads," Pete said.

"So do you."

Carly curled her fingers over Reese's knee. "I'll help him," she said. "I'll have time."

That ended that conversation, and Kelly moved on to opening presents. Carly and Reese faded into the background, but she didn't mind, and he didn't seem to either. He held her hand, occasionally lifting her fingers to his lips, and smiled at the kids, and avoided adult conversation by helping Kelly's father clean the grill.

By the end of the party, he wore exhaustion on his face. She felt it way down deep in her bones, and they left first. She rode next to him in his truck, the conversation she wanted to have blocked behind a film of uncertainty. She didn't want to ruin her time with him with serious talk about their future together.

She wasn't even sure they had a future together.

He pulled into his driveway and killed the engine but stayed in his seat. He stared at the house like it contained secrets, or answers, or both.

"My interview is on Thursday," she said. "I'm not leaving until that morning. I'm going to come home the same day." She took a deep breath, memorizing the scent of leather and musk that personified his truck. "Then I don't have to pay for a hotel room."

He swung toward her, something burning in his dark eyes. "Do you want the job?"

"I *need* a job," she said. "Did Lindsay call you last week?"

He shook his head. "No one called. Pete said they didn't call him either."

A frown crept across her face. "That doesn't seem right. Lindsay said she was going to call you."

Reese slid his arm around her shoulders, pulling her close and touching his lips to her forehead, then her nose, then her lips. His slow and steady kiss ignited a fire deep inside her, reminding her why she didn't want the job in Oklahoma City.

"You want to come in?" he asked. "I ordered a lot of ice cream last time I went to the grocery store."

She laughed, and he slid out of the truck, keeping his hand in hers. He left the front door open, only letting the screen crash closed behind them. A warm breeze drifted into the house, a welcome visitor, as Carly sat on the couch. Reese returned a few minutes later with two bowls full of cookies 'n cream.

"No lime sherbet?"

"You know, I tried to order some, but they were plumb out." He grinned as he put a bite of ice cream in his mouth. "Turns out, no one likes it so they stopped making it."

"Oh, be quiet." She gave him a playful shove as he chuckled. The sound morphed into a groan of genuine pain, and Carly's eyes widened. "Reese, I'm sorry. Did I hurt you?"

He ground his teeth together as he set his bowl on the coffee table in front of him. "It's just...." He trailed off and dropped his gaze to the floor so she couldn't judge how much pain he was in. From the way he gasped for air, she concluded she'd really hurt him.

"I hit you where the horse stepped on you, didn't I?" She set aside her own bowl of ice cream, her appetite suddenly gone.

"It's fine," he said through clenched teeth. "I'll be fine in a second."

But it took a lot longer than a second for him to recover.

"What can I do?" Carly got up and turned toward the kitchen. Maybe he had some painkillers left over from a couple of months ago.

"Nothing. Sit down." He leaned against the back of the couch, his eyes closed. His skin looked like wet cement, and a bead of sweat trailed down the side of his face. As he breathed, life came back into his complexion, and he opened his eyes. "See? Just fine."

"You're not fine," she said. "And I—"

A spark of anger edged his irises. "You're right. I'm not fine. But this is who I am. I will never be whole again. Never."

Carly flinched with the force of his words. "I didn't say—"

"It doesn't matter what you say," he said. "I can see everything in your face. You think I didn't see you watching Squire at the birthday party?"

Her eyebrows drew together. "I don't know what you mean."

"You were watchin' him and Finn play. I saw the fondness on

your face. And you should know, Carly, that I can never give you that. I won't be able to run and play with our kids."

She sucked in a breath at the thought of having a family, a future, with him. "I don't care about that."

He chuckled, but this one sounded harsh and grating. "Right. I *saw* you."

"And I just saw you!" She stood up. "And you're not fine."

He reached for his ice cream and limped into the kitchen, calling, "Yes, I am," over his shoulder.

"I should go." Carly reached for her purse and fumbled for her keys. "Thank you for the ice cream."

He remained in the kitchen, leaning against the counter with a glowering expression she felt across the distance between them. As she left, she wondered why he needed to put this wall between them, now of all times.

Because she didn't care about his physical limitations. She never once had. Never even thought about them until that evening. She understood his frustration, his anger, over his condition. As she drove through the sleepy town toward her house, the sting he'd given her lessened.

She pulled in her driveway and sent him a text. *Lunch tomorrow?*

He didn't answer, and the thrum of rejection strummed through her again.

---

THURSDAY MORNING DAWNED WITH THE PROMISE OF A HOT DAY— and with a continued cold shoulder from Reese. She'd texted him several times, and he'd responded with one-word answers.

*No.*

*Yes.*

*Can't.*

*Tomorrow.*

She silenced her phone as she set her car east, settling in for the three and a half hour drive. With the radio on loud enough to drown out her self-deprecating thoughts, she arrived at the school before she knew it.

She smoothed her blouse as she headed up the sidewalk, her heartbeat bobbing against the back of her tongue. Once inside the building, though, her thoughts quieted. Her fear subsided.

James Yancey, the director, met her at the door to the office, a slight man in his early fifties, she guessed.

"Doctor Yancey." She shook his hand and smiled. He welcomed her to Hollyhock House and asked her how the drive from Texas had gone. They made small talk about her family, and the students at Hollyhock, and with the first lull in the conversation, Carly pulled her resume and work experience out of her briefcase bag.

"You'll see I have three years' experience with a public clinic in Amarillo," she said. "I earned my Master's degree and passed my boards just last year."

Doctor Yancey glanced at her meticulously prepared documents, barely scanning them long enough to read them. "Why do you want to work with kids?" he asked.

Carly's mind raced. "I like helping people," she said. "Most recently, I've been assisting veterans as part of the State Veteran Care Program. Kids will actually be easy compared to that." She gave a light laugh, silencing herself when Doctor Yancey barely smiled.

"Our children require a great deal of attention," he said. "Are you planning to relocate to Oklahoma City?"

"Yes, sir."

He fingered her folder again but didn't pick it up. "Their parents need an immense amount of help with insurance, educational paperwork, and Individualized Education Plans. Are you familiar with an IEP?"

"No, sir," Carly said. "But I can learn anything I need to. I'm very good at finding services for people who need them. It would be an honor to help children and their families navigate the systems to find and receive the assistance they need."

The rest of the interview went just fine, but when Carly left, a heavy feeling in her stomach told her Hollyhock wasn't the right place for her. She knew it in the back of her mind, but dismissed the thought, telling herself instead that she needed a good job. One that paid enough to pay her student loans—and gas money to Three Rivers and back once a week.

Hollyhock provided that. And it would be the easiest job by far. The others in the city were all in healthcare, and the paperwork there would make her job now seem like nothing.

Still, she drove by Saint Anthony's and inquired about a job. The woman at the reception desk gave her a card with a website on it, and Carly tucked it into her purse for the long ride back to Three Rivers.

Reese skipped work on Thursday completely. It was the day after the Fourth, and most of the cowhands had the day off. Everything on the ranch sat in hazy heat as Reese made his way over to Pete's homestead.

He knocked on the front door at the same time he entered.

Pete turned from his position at the stove, where the smell of pancakes met Reese's nose.

"I'm ready to ride again," Reese announced.

Pete's eyebrows rose, but without his cowboy hat on, he couldn't hide the surprise in his eyes. "You are?"

"Yep. Maybe this evening, after it cools off?"

"Sure thing." Pete turned back to the stove. "You eat breakfast yet?"

"Nope." He didn't tell Pete he didn't actually eat breakfast as the lieutenant dished him three pancakes and nudged the syrup closer to where he'd settled at the bar.

"Where's Chelsea and Julie?"

"They went over to Kelly's," Pete said. "Guess the women are all goin' shopping today."

A flash of worry wormed through Reese, though he wasn't sure why he cared if Chelsea, Kelly, and Kate went shopping. Other than that it left him alone on the ranch with the men—all of whom certainly had some advice for Reese about Carly.

Sure enough, Pete said, "So what's goin' on with you and Carly?"

Reese stuffed his mouth full of pancake so he couldn't answer.

"Ah, breakfast." Brett walked through the sliding glass door and into the dining room. He picked up a plate from the stack on the counter and held it out for Pete to put on the next hot pancakes.

"Squire comin'?"

"He's about two minutes behind me. He was helpin' Finn and Reid find their shoes." He shook his head. "I told him little boys don't need shoes, but the major insisted." He sat at the counter next to Reese. "Hey. How's things?"

That was all Brett had to say to ask every question under the sun. "Great," Reese said. "I'm gonna ride again tonight."

Brett didn't miss a beat as he forked a slab of pancake into his mouth. "Great. Yeah. Which horse?"

He glanced at Pete, but the other man didn't turn from the griddle. "Probably Peony."

"She misses you," Pete said without turning.

"Maybe Arrowhead."

Squire came through the door leading to the garage, both little boys in tow. Reese watched them get loaded up with pancakes and syrup, watched Squire get them seated at the bar and pour them plastic cups of orange juice. He thought about his own ability to help his kids one day. He wanted to do it—like he wanted to walk normally and not get tired after a half hour of walking—but he knew he'd always be a burden to whoever he married. He couldn't help it if Carly's face filled his mind when he pictured his wife.

"Where's Carly this mornin'?" Squire asked as he flanked Reese on his other side. "Kelly said she called her, but she said she couldn't go shopping today."

"She's in Oklahoma City," Reese said, deciding to get the inevitable out of the way. "She has a job interview this morning at a special-needs school."

Brett finished his pancakes and swallowed a mouthful of coffee. "That's great. I mean, is that great?" He glanced at the other men, and Reese felt a flicker of a bond with Brett. Brett, who because he lived so far away, didn't know all the gossip, wasn't involved in everything that happened at Three Rivers.

"No, it's not great," Squire spoke for Reese. "He's in love with the woman, and—"

"Whoa," Reese said, his heart booming. "I'm not in love with her."

Pete poured a healthy amount of syrup on his short stack. "Not yet."

Reese glared, but didn't argue.

"Point is," Squire said, reaching for the sugar and adding a spoonful to his coffee. "She can't live and work in Oklahoma City when Reese lives and works here."

"Long-distance things sometimes work," Brett said.

"She's the first woman he's even so much as taken a second look at," Pete said as if Reese wasn't even in the room. "He'll find a way to make it work." He gave Squire a look that said, *Leave it be.*

"What if I don't want it to work out?" The silence after Reese's question made the other three men pause. Though his family was miles away, his six older brothers far from Three Rivers, Reese had never felt as seventh best as he did in that moment.

"What do you mean you don't want it to work out?" Pete asked.

Reese shrugged, though his insecurities loitered so close to the surface. Too close. "She deserves someone better than me."

Brett held up his hand as Pete opened his mouth to say something. He glanced back at Reese. "What does that mean?"

He pushed his sticky pancake around on his nearly-full plate. "I don't know."

"Yes, you do," Brett insisted. "Spill it, Sergeant."

"It means I don't want to saddle her with a life of taking care of me." As soon as Reese spoke, he realized how true the words rang in his ears. They seemed deafening in the cavernous kitchen, the walls capturing the syllables and echoing them back to him over and over.

He struggled against the seemingly ever-present frustration, helpless to push back the feelings of self-pity and self-loathing that came so easily.

"So...she lost her job because of me. Well, not yet." He shoved his plate away. "But she will lose her job. And...I don't know. I don't have anything to offer her but this life." And while it was a life he loved, he couldn't imagine raising a family on his simple salary, in his one-bedroom house. He didn't have a homestead on a sprawling ranch. He didn't have a doctorate degree. He didn't have his own business.

He had his life, but he couldn't imagine a smart, beautiful, capable woman like Carly wanting it. Wanting him.

"Well, give her a chance," Pete said. "Women have a way of healing broken things."

Brett put his hand on Reese's forearm, drawing his attention to the other man's face. "Seriously, Reese. Don't push her away."

Reese wondered how Brett had known that was exactly what Reese had tried to do. He thought perhaps the agony of losing her would be easier if she didn't want to be with him, if she didn't stick by his side through thick and thin.

The sliding glass door opened again, and Garth folded his broad cowboy shoulders through them. "Hey, am I too late for breakfast? Juliette forgot to tell me about the festivities."

Pete got up from the bar and started the fire under the griddle. "Lots left, Garth. How's Juliette feeling?"

"Well enough to go to Amarillo for the day." He poured himself a cup of coffee and caught Reese's eye. "Could use an extra hand in the horse barn today. You in?"

The idea of spending time with creatures who couldn't talk appealed to Reese. "Sure."

"Great. Most of the cowhands are gone today. Only me and Ethan to do the essentials."

"We're takin' the kids to the swimming hole," Squire said. "But if you're not done when we get back, we'll help."

Reese listened to Garth talk about Juliette's pregnancy, and Squire discuss what he and Kelly were going to name their little girl, and Pete probe Brett for more information about his kids riding camp. As he sat with the other men, he wondered if he could leave Three Rivers and follow Carly to Oklahoma City.

He wasn't sure if he could. He loved these men, had served with men like them, and they loved him. Whole, broken, or in-between, they loved him.

He wondered if Carly could too.

The horse barn held stuffy air scented by manure and hay. Reese inhaled the smell, regretting his time away from the animals he loved. Peony met him at the fence, and he bent to press his forehead to her nose.

She snuffled at him, her way of saying hello. An overwhelming pulse of peace pushed through him, silencing his fears, his failures, his frustrations. And he knew in that moment, that he couldn't leave Three Rivers, not even for Carly Watters.

He took a deep breath and closed his eyes, the thought of a prayer rotating through his mind. No words formed besides a sincere *Thank you, Lord.*

"They need to be fed." Garth's voice broke Reese's reverie, and he stepped away from Peony's stall.

"We'll ride later," he promised her, and she closed her eyes halfway in acceptance.

That evening, after Reese had spent a few hours working on the ranch, and then a few hours resting in the basement of the homestead, he returned to the barn to saddle Peony. Pete met him at the entrance to the outdoor arena, and Reese's feet suddenly stalled.

The last time he'd been on Peony in this arena, his world had turned upside down. A phantom ache spread down his leg from his hip and up into his chest, where Peony had stomped on him.

She waited next to him, her head hung low. Pete stared into the dusky sky, seemingly without a care in the world.

Reese took a deep breath, wishing he'd been able to talk to Carly this afternoon. She'd said she'd call, but she hadn't. He wondered how her interview had gone. Wondered if she really wanted to be with him. Wondered if she'd stay in Three Rivers if he asked her to.

He released the air in his lungs and took a step into the arena. Peony dutifully came with him, held as still as a statue as he lined up the step-stool so he could get in the saddle. Pete appeared at his side like a shadow, silent but present.

Reese managed to mount the horse without assistance, though he was glad Pete stood nearby just in case. He gripped the reins too tight, like he had the first time he'd come out to Three Rivers to ride.

"Steady," Pete said. "Gentle."

A bolt of lightning shot down Reese's back and his abs felt like gelatin that hadn't had enough time to set in the refrigerator. Maybe he wasn't quite ready to be on a horse again.

He released the tension in his grip and clucked his tongue at Peony. She moved forward at the speed of a sloth, but it felt like a gallop to Reese. Was riding this hard the first time? He couldn't quite remember. He did know it would get easier the more he did it, and he vowed to ride Peony every day, if only for a few minutes.

He circled the arena once, his breath coming quicker with the effort it took to hold himself on her back, to sit up straight.

"You okay?" Pete called from his position on the fence. The man had a maddening ability to read both horses and men, even from a distance, even when not a sound was made.

"Fine," Reese called, thinking of how Carly would react if she heard him say *fine*.

"That's what he always says."

Reese startled at the sound of her voice, and he searched for her along the fence line. She stood at the entrance to the arena, her elbows draped lazily over the top rung as she balanced her sneakered feet on the bottom rung.

He felt self-conscious in the saddle, with her watching him from the ground. "What are you doing here?" he called.

"Came to see you. Couldn't find you at your place. Thought you'd be here." She grinned in his direction, and his heart flopped against his ribcage. Had she gotten the job and come to celebrate? Or not, and she needed support? He couldn't tell from the smile on her face, the way she painted over all her emotions so easily.

He directed Peony with his feet, the way he'd been taught. The steady clomping of her hooves soothed him, even with Carly's gaze solidly on his back. He gazed into the bruising sky, his soul quiet and his mind settled. Finally.

After a couple more circuits around the arena, he moved Peony to the stool still in the middle of the circle. Pete met him there, ready to help if needed. He didn't crowd, but when Reese stumbled on the dismount, he caught him by the bicep.

"Easy," he said. "Find your feet."

But Reese couldn't. His feet felt numb. "Pete." He gripped the other man's arm. "Don't let go."

"What's—?"

"I can't feel my feet." Tingles raced up his legs, shooting sparks through his hip. "Pete, I can't feel my feet."

## 14

Carly kept her fingers fisted around the steering wheel as she drove the now familiar two-lane road into town. In the passenger seat, Reese sat staring out the window, his head supported by his right hand. They hadn't spoken past her offer to take him to the hospital and Pete saying he'd follow in his truck.

She pulled into the emergency room parking lot, cut the engine, and hurried around to Reese's side. He didn't try to get out, and she couldn't help him until Pete arrived with Reese's wheelchair.

She crouched in the space created by the open door. "Reese," she said, her voice rusty from its many hours of silence.

"You should go home, Carly."

Disbelief tore through her. She'd driven to Oklahoma City and back in one day, and gone straight to him. And he wanted her to go home? "I'm not going anywhere."

"Pete will call my dad. He'll come in the morning. I'll be—" He cut off at her intense glare. At least he hadn't said *fine* yet.

A sliver of worry seethed with intense frustration. "Reese, I'm not leaving you here."

"I don't want you here."

She glared, her anger rearing. "Too bad."

Thankfully, Pete pulled in, silencing Reese's next comment. Carly had honored his foul mood the first time he was hurt. When he said he didn't want her there, she'd given him space. But it had been almost three months. She'd barely known him then. Now, she'd kissed him, and she liked him, and she would not abandon him, even though he'd asked her to.

She paced to the back of the car, where Pete waited. "How is he?"

Carly ran her hand through her hair and exhaled. "He's grumpy."

"Ask you to leave him alone?"

She hated how Pete peered at her, like he could see past her perfectly painted lips and artfully made-up eyes to the real emotion teeming underneath. "Yeah."

"Don't you do it, Miss Carly. He'll come around."

Carly's eyes turned hot as tears crowded forward. "Am I just supposed to take that from him?" she asked. "Why does he say such hurtful things?"

Pete's intense expression softened. "It's the only way he knows how to protect himself. He doesn't really want you to leave."

Carly nodded, but the gruffness of Reese's voice still ripped through her insides, shredding the previous places the sergeant had started to heal.

"I'll talk to him." Pete started toward the front of Carly's car.

She held up her palm. "I don't need you to do that." She turned and moved back to Reese. "Pete has your wheelchair." She opened the door as far as it would go and stepped behind the wheelchair to hold it steady.

She watched as Reese lifted his legs over the shallow lip of her car and set his feet on the asphalt. He didn't seem to be in pain, but he moved slowly, like his legs were encased in quicksand.

His mouth pressed together in a determined line, and she admired his strength and iron will. He used the car's frame to support himself as he stood. The absolute steel in his expression set Carly's heartbeat to pounding, and she'd never found a man so desirable.

"What?" he asked as he caught her eye.

"Nothing." The word scratched out of her throat, filled with emotion.

He kicked her a half-smile and sat in the chair. "I can feel my toes a little now."

"Let's go see what the doctor says," Pete said.

Carly didn't give Reese a choice. She pulled him backward and Pete slammed the car door and together they went into the emergency room.

An hour later, Reese claimed that his legs and feet were fine. He got up and paced the small space in the curtained-off area where Carly sat, waiting for the doctor to come back. He'd seen Reese fairly quickly, asked a slew of questions, taken a CT scan of Reese's spine, and left him and Carly alone in the tiny area.

"So what do you think happened?" she asked.

Pete had left after the doctor had called Reese back, and Carly had promised to update him. She thumbed out a message that Reese's paralysis seemed to have abated, but that they were waiting on results from the scan and to talk to the doctor.

"Maybe something with riding the horse?" Reese guessed, coming back to the bed. He sat down. "I'm real sorry about saying I didn't want you here. I...do want you here."

She glanced up from her phone to find his gaze as earnest as she'd ever seen it. "Why do you do that then?"

He folded his hands in his lap and studied them, a flush rising through his neck. "I'm embarrassed. I want to be strong for you, for us. I want to...." He trailed off and shrugged. "I don't know." He glanced up. "I'm trying."

She leaned forward and gathered his hands in hers. "Apology accepted. But, you know, Sergeant, there might be a day where you tell me to leave, and I won't come back." Her words surprised her, especially after the strength of feelings she'd had for him in the parking lot.

"I know," he said. "My friends keep tellin' me that. Tellin' me not to push you away."

"You have smart friends." She released his hands and sat back. "You should listen to them."

Reese turned stony after that, and Carly didn't push him. He had apologized, and she'd accepted it. But as the minutes ticked by, she wondered *why* she was willing to accept it. The answer came almost immediately: She liked Reese Sanders, and she wanted to help him.

A shiver of fear accompanied the thought. Could her desire to help him, serve him, spend time with him, grow into love for him?

As she watched him get up and pace again, she knew she could fall in love with him. She bit her lip, wondering if he could ever love her too. She'd never let anyone besides Tanner in far enough to find out, and he'd taken who she was and thrown it away like last week's trash.

"You okay?" Reese asked, drawing Carly out of the dregs of her self-esteem.

"Yeah," she said, putting on a bright smile.

He frowned, and a blip of fear stole through her. *Blip, blip.*

"Why do you do that?" he asked.

"Do what?" She blinked at him.

"Say you're okay when you're not." He seemed to be able to see past all her carefully crafted exteriors—the ones that kept her mom from giving unwanted advice and her sisters from knowing how much she envied them.

"Must've learned it from you." She grinned, hoping he'd drop the subject. "After all, you're *fine*."

He looked like she'd tossed a bucket of icy water in his face. Then he tipped his head back and laughed. The sound hurtled through Carly's ears, burrowed into her soul. She wanted to hear him laugh without restraint over and over again.

"I guess we both do it," he said. "Probably should work on being more honest with each other." He took a deep breath and sat on the end of the bed again. "How was the job interview?"

Before she could answer, the doctor pulled back the curtain and entered the space. "CT scan is back." He smiled. "Great news. No nerve damage, Reese. But the sciatic is enflamed." He switched on a light and stuck the films to the clips along the top of the box. "My guess is while you were riding, that nerve—" He pointed to a white spot with radiating tentacles. "Got all squished around. It cut off blood flow to your feet, and that caused the paralysis. Temporary paralysis."

Relief rushed through Carly with the doctor's explanation. She hadn't realized how tense he'd been until she watched the tight lines around his gorgeous eyes soften, the tic in his jaw disappear, the clenched nature of his fists release. She reached over and threaded her fingers through his, glad when he squeezed back.

"So can I go?" he asked.

"Feeling better?"

He practically leapt off the bed. "Yes. Look, I can walk and everything."

The doctor made a note on Reese's chart. "Then, yes. You're free to go. Maybe see if Pete has an extra-high saddle for you. That'll keep your back straighter by pushing up higher on your lower back. That should keep the sciatic from getting pinched again."

Reese nodded, tucked his hand back into Carly's, and headed for the exit.

Carly drove home, her words rushing out of her in a near-babble. She told him about the interview, the drive around to hospitals, the trip home.

"And I just know I won't get that job," she said as she pulled into his driveway. "I didn't feel good there."

"But you said the interview went great."

"It did. But I won't get the job." She knew it like she knew the sun was hot. "I've got lots more options. And Lindsay hasn't even called yet."

Reese half-turned toward her. "Why do you think that is?"

Carly shrugged, though the fact that Lindsay hadn't called sent a pop of anxiety down to her toes.

"You want to come in?" he asked as he reached for the door handle.

"It's late," she said, glancing at the digital clock on her radio. "I should get home."

"Just for a half hour." His gaze burned right through her. "I just want another half hour with you. One where I'm not paralyzed or in the hospital."

She couldn't contain the grin that spread her lips, or the heat that pressed against her lungs at his strong, deep voice.

As she strolled up the steps with him, the words reorganized themselves into *I want you*. He closed the door behind them, and Carly hadn't taken a single step before he pulled her into his chest.

"Right here, beautiful. I want you right here." He kissed her, and she felt the depth of his feelings as his strong arms encircled her. For the first time in a long time, she felt cherished, adored, safe. She felt like she could be herself, and Reese wouldn't mind. She could wear sweatpants, and he'd think her desirable. She could confess her darkest fears, and he'd hold her and help her find her way through them.

She returned his kiss, deepening it, pressing closer so as to not miss a moment of being with him.

---

REESE STOOD JUST TO THE LEFT OF THE WINDOW, WATCHING AS Carly pranced down his sidewalk. His motion-sensor lights bathed her in white light, bounced off her hair, illuminated her smile as she glanced back to the house before getting in her car.

She couldn't see him, but he grinned too. Kissing her felt like having his full strength back, like he could be whole again with her in his arms. He switched off the lights and limped down the hall to his bedroom, determined never to push her away again. If she wanted to see the ugliness of his life, he'd let her.

Truth was, he *wanted* her to see it. Wanted her to know what she was getting herself into by continuing a relationship with him. Again, his thoughts toyed with the idea of marriage, and again, he shut himself down before he could allow hope to seep through his bloodstream. He knew hope was both beneficial and dangerous. It gave a man ideas about things he ought not consider until a more appropriate time.

And just because Carly let him kiss her whenever he wanted —and she seemed to like it a whole lot—didn't mean he should be thinkin' of marrying her. But his heart didn't seem to get that message, and it continued to beat out constant streams of nuptials as he fell asleep. He couldn't even escape himself while he slept, because his dreams featured the gorgeous blonde who'd unexpectedly shown up in his life and turned it upside down.

He woke with the sun streaming through his windows, his mind refreshed, but his lower back aching like he'd been backed over by a tractor. He groaned as he rolled himself out of bed. His first thought was to call Carly, and his second was to dismiss the first.

He remembered her cool demeanor at the hospital, the way

he'd hurt her by telling her to go home. He needed to break down the walls between them—the walls he'd built—if he wanted to keep her in his life.

As he contemplated what he wanted, he couldn't imagine a future without her in it. So he padded down the hall without brushing his teeth—his morning breath wouldn't transmit through a phone call—and dialed her.

"Reese?" she answered. "What happened?"

His insides twisted at her assumption. "I guess I need to call you more. Nothin's wrong."

Her relieved exhale annoyed him for a reason he couldn't name. Yes, he could. His own stubbornness over the past several weeks of *not* calling her when he wanted to. Why had he done that?

"Well, what's going on?" she asked.

"Just wanted to hear your voice." He sat at the bar. "I'm actually thinking about eating breakfast today, and I was hopin' you'd join me."

She giggled, the girlish sound tickling his eardrums and eliciting a smile.

"Is that a yes?"

"As long as you're paying," she said. "I don't want to foot the bill for waffles you won't eat."

"Hey," he protested, but he found he couldn't vocalize another suitable argument. "Okay, you're right. I'll probably just have a cup of coffee."

She agreed to meet him at Betty Sue's Pancake House in an hour, and he went down the hall, whistling, to shower. He'd made it to his bedroom when his phone buzzed again. He slid it on without checking who it was.

"Miss me already?"

Someone cleared their throat. "Is this Sergeant Sanders?"

Reese froze. He checked the phone, but didn't recognize the number. "It is."

"This is Lindsay Miner. I'm the director at the Amarillo South Center. We've been providing veteran care services for you for a few years?"

The blood in Reese's veins turned to ice. "Yes, ma'am," he managed to say.

"I have a few questions for you about your current care coordinator, Carly Watters. Do you have a few minutes?"

Reese had no choice. He took the few steps to the recliner in his bedroom and sat down. "I sure do."

"Very well. Let's begin back in April, when Miss Watters first came to Three Rivers...."

———

REESE'S FOUL MOOD BECAUSE OF THE PHONE CALL THAT FELT LIKE an interrogation followed him to breakfast. Thirty minutes late, he limped up the steps and into the diner. Sandy, the hostess, met him with a smile and a menu. "Hey, Reese. Just you?"

"I'm meeting someone," he said. "She's been here a while...." He scanned the pancake house for Carly's angelic hair and couldn't find her.

"Carly?" Sandy asked.

Reese focused on her, relief flooding him. He appreciated the glint in her eye as she swept him from his boots to his cowboy hat. "Yeah, Carly."

"She's in the corner." She pointed behind her to the left, and Reese flashed her a quick smile of thanks when he caught a glimpse of Carly's face.

"I'm so sorry I'm late," he said as he slid into the booth opposite of her. She'd already ordered, and the biggest country breakfast Reese had ever seen spread out on the table in front of her. His stomach squeezed.

"You texted," she said. "It's no problem."

The waitress approached, and Reese requested coffee with

cream and sugar. She brought his mug only a few seconds later. His mind churned over how to start the conversation. In the end, he simply blurted, "Lindsay called. That's why I was late."

She paused with her forkful of hashbrowns halfway to her mouth. "Lindsay called this morning?"

"Yeah." He scrubbed the back of his head, dislodging his cowboy hat. It pushed forward, over his eyes.

Carly reached over and took his hat in her hand. He lifted his eyes to hers and stared at her. He felt like everything between them blew wide open, with her holding his hat and him staring at her.

"I told her everything," he said, though he couldn't tell her certain parts of the conversation. "No point in lyin' about it." Though, as he'd spoken with Lindsay and told her about his relationship with Carly, he'd realized something.

He was in deep. Too deep to get out now. And he didn't *want* to get out now.

"What did she say?" Carly abandoned her food, her attention on him singular.

"She asked a lot of questions. Kept saying, 'I see,' and asking something else. In the end, she said she'd be in touch if she needed anything else. That was it."

Carly reached a shaking hand toward her orange juice. Reese captured it in his and drew it to his lips. "Hey, it's okay," he said. "We knew she was going to call. You're prepared to...." He cut himself off before he could say something insensitive. A fierce rush of love for her flowed through him when she steadied the wobble in her chin and gripped his fingers with a strength he wished he had.

"I am prepared," she said. "I'm going to lose my job, but it's okay."

"Carly, I'm real sorry." He felt like all he ever did was apologize to her. He glanced away, wishing the inadequacy igniting in his gut would go out.

"It's not your fault," she said. "I kissed you back. I *wanted* to kiss you back."

He ducked his head despite not being able to hide behind his hat. "That's nice to hear, beautiful. Because I don't want to regret kissin' you." He met her gaze. "I'd walk around that Tulip Festival everyday if it meant I could kiss you every night before I fall asleep."

Her eyes searched his, but he didn't think she found what she was looking for. "I don't think I was terribly unprofessional," she said. "I took care of your needs, filled out your hospital forms, spent time with you." Her voice wouldn't convince anyone, but Reese didn't need to be persuaded.

Her phone rang, and she startled. Glancing at the screen, she sucked in a breath. "It's Lindsay."

"You should take it," he said.

She grabbed the phone and bolted to standing. She swiped open the call as she headed for the exit without a backward glance. He watched her climb into her purple car, her mouth moving a mile a minute. He wasn't sure what to do: Wait here for her to return? Pick up the check and hang out in his truck until she finished her phone call?

In the end, he sipped his coffee in an attempt to calm his raging stomach. It didn't work. He ordered a Western omelet, thinking maybe food would help ease the queasiness inside. But as soon as the waitress set the steaming plate of eggs and ham in front of him, he felt like throwing up. No way he could put that in his mouth.

"I changed my mind," he said, calling her back. "Can I get this to go?"

"Sure thing, honey." She picked up the plate. "Is Miss Carly gonna want hers?"

Reese scanned the half-eaten hashbrowns, the untouched pancakes, the cold scrambled eggs. "Yeah, can you box it all up? Then I just need the check."

"No problem." She moved back toward the kitchen, returning a moment later with his omelet boxed and a couple of boxes for Carly's food. She made quick work of putting it in containers and placing the receipt on the table.

"Thanks, Jean." He stood, pulled his wallet out of his back pocket, and went to pay the bill. Though Carly still spoke on the phone, her free hand gesturing into the empty space around her, Reese slid into her passenger seat.

"...my forwarding address." She glanced at him and he gave her an encouraging smile.

"Yes, that's fine, Lindsay. I really am sorry. Okay. Yes. Good-bye." She ended the call and stared out the window.

"I boxed up your food, beautiful."

She twisted toward him. "Let's go somewhere."

"Where?"

She jammed her keys into the ignition. "Anywhere. Let's just drive until we feel like getting out of the car, and then let's find something to do. You game for a little adventure?"

He lifted his eyebrows at her. Brett was leaving tomorrow, and Reese did want to pick his brain about the kids' riding camp. But he knew Brett's number. He could call him later.

"I guess I won't be goin' to work today."

She laughed, but it sounded a bit on the maniacal side. "Not today, Sergeant."

## 15

C arly felt numb, though the steering wheel beneath her fingers felt solid, and the radio in the car blasted too loudly for comfort, and the smell of Reese mixing with bacon and salsa almost had her pulling over so she could taste him.

"How'd the phone call go?"

She noticed he gripped the armrest with more force than he normally did. She aimed the car south and checked the gas gauge. Three-quarters of a tank. They could get good and lost out here in the Texas Panhandle with that much gas.

"I was right," she said as she accelerated. "I lost my job. They're giving me two months of severance pay, though, and there will be no formal reprimand. Nothing on my record that says I was inappropriate with a client."

Her fingers released their grip on the wheel, though her insides still coiled like an angry cobra. "Whatever you said to Lindsay was the right thing. She didn't find me to be inappropriate in my social work for you, and though her recommendation had to be termination, I got off easy."

A barking sound came out of her throat she supposed could be classified as laughter. Why, then, did she feel like sobbing?

"Pull over, beautiful." His soft voice undid her composure. Tears leaked out the corners of her eyes as she eased onto the shoulder.

With the car stopped and in park, he gathered her close and held her. She pressed her cheek over his heartbeat and let herself cry. "I'm sorry," she said. "I don't know why I'm so upset."

"It's okay." He stroked her hair, and she adored the warmth in his touch, his voice, his body. "Don't apologize."

He gave her the time she needed to quiet herself, then he said, "Two months severance is good, right?"

It was good, but it didn't ease the pressure against her lungs, the band that seemed ever-present around her chest, the ache pulsing behind her eyes. She hated crying.

"It is," she confirmed. "But I still need a new job."

"Maybe the major can find you something at the ranch."

"What's a social worker going to do on a ranch?"

He pressed his lips to her temple. She tightened her grip around his strong back.

"Not sure, my love."

She pulled back at the endearment, at the tender catch in his voice. She examined him for any hint of a lie, any indication whatsoever that his words were only made of letters.

"I'll put your position on the remaining grants I haven't sent in yet. They don't normally provide even half of what you need for your salary, but it's worth a try, right?" He spoke in a calm, steady way, and she marveled at this new man in front of her. She thought of the first time she'd met him, the way he'd wandered through the barn and whispered to the horses. He was that strong, confident man then, and the same one sat in her car now.

"It's worth a try," she said. "Thank you." She took a steadying breath and leaned toward him, suddenly anxious to have his lips on hers, see if she could feel the love he'd almost professed for her.

She could feel something. Something good, and strong, and worth having. As she kissed him, she felt herself falling further down the like line and into love. The thought scared her as much as being unemployed in a Texas town with only one grocery store.

He cupped her face in his hands, removing his mouth from hers, but barely. "We'll get through this," he whispered. "Me and you. Together."

Oh, how she adored this man. "Me and you," she repeated. "Together. Does that go both ways?"

A flicker of fear stole through his beautiful dark diamond eyes. "Yep," he said. "Both ways." The moment between them broke, and Reese relaxed into his seat. "Now I think you said something about an adventure today."

An hour later, she pulled into an empty parking lot after having seen a sign proclaiming, "We Brought the Buffalo Back."

"Buffalo," she said, feigning excitement for Reese. She peered out the windshield. "Look. It's the Charles Goodnight house." She looked at him. "Do you know who Charles Goodnight is?"

"Should I?" He seemed a bit dubious that this somewhat plain house was going to be their adventure.

She slid him a smile and got out of the car. The wind tore through her hair like it had a personal vendetta against her. "Come on," she said as he got out much slower than her. "He's the Father of American Ranching. You should know who he is."

Reese rolled his eyes. "So I can sit behind a counter and make appointments?"

"You work on a *ranch*." Carly tucked her arm in his as they moved toward the obviously renovated house. "You should know about the Father of American Ranching."

He pressed his lips to her temple as they went up the steps. "Okay, beautiful."

A smiling tour guide met them at the door, and Carly's spirits lifted. The sixty-minute ride with Reese's hand in hers had helped. But a constant storm cloud kept infiltrating her thoughts. Out here, though, with nothing surrounding this lonely stretch of highway for miles and miles, she allowed her cares and worries to evaporate into the bright blue sky.

She admired the displays of original wallpaper, the replicas of an era gone by. She stood on the back porch of Charles Goodnight's house and tried to picture what Texas would've looked like a hundred and fifty years ago.

*Probably about the same*, she thought, and her lips curved up.

"We have a bison herd here again," the tour guide said as she held out a pair of binoculars. "If we're lucky, we'll get to see them in the distance. Charles bred buffalo with cattle, resulting in what he called cattalo."

"Cattalo," Carly repeated, a laugh bubbling in the back of her throat. She let it out, feeling the last of her doldrums disappear. "That's funny." She held the binoculars to her eyes, searching for a distant, brown dot on the horizon.

"I see them!" She jammed the binoculars at Reese. "Look!"

He obliged, claimed he saw them, and handed the binoculars back to the tour guide.

"Well, that completes the tour," she said. "Here in Goodnight, we like to say 'goodnight to all' no matter what time of day it is."

"Goodnight," Carly said, glad when Reese said it too, though an hour remained until lunchtime.

"Where to now?" she asked once they'd buckled themselves back in her car.

"Somewhere with more than eighteen people for a population," he said. "And you thought Three Rivers was small. This place doesn't even have a gas station."

"Five thousand isn't a big population either."

"Hey," he said. "Three Rivers has almost *fifteen* thousand people."

"It does not." She glanced at him. "No way one grocery store supports that many people."

"It does," he said. "I looked it up after you complained about the tininess of the town. And we used to have two grocery stores. One closed last summer."

She clucked her tongue like he'd just proven her point, but she didn't know what point that was.

"The owner died, and his son didn't want the store."

"But he was doing well?"

"Sure," Reese said. "He'd been open for years, from what I understand."

Carly's brain whirred around the information, but she quickly dismissed the insane ideas in her head. She didn't want to open a grocery store. She didn't even know the first thing about such a thing.

"Okay, so a bigger town," she said, swiping on her phone to open her map app. "South? North? East? West?" She glanced at him. "Which way do you want to go?"

"West," he said decisively.

"We can't really go west from here," she said, studying her screen. "We'd have to go all the way back to Amarillo." And she didn't want to do that. The city she'd thought she'd never leave didn't seem to hold anything for her anymore. Returning felt like a giant step backward.

"East, then, I guess. What's that way?"

"Wellington is about an hour away. Small...but hey, look." She tilted the phone toward him, but didn't give him much of a chance to see it. "There's a Historic Ritz Theater. It was a national finalist in the 'This Place Matters' contest."

"Better go see that," he mused. "It must matter if it was a finalist."

"There's a diner, too," she said. "Looks like burgers and fries."

"I like burgers and fries."

Carly put the car in drive, glad to have an escape from her life, even for a few hours. Even happier to be spending the time and adventure with Reese. Though she wouldn't admit it to herself, she felt like today might be all they had left. The fact remained that she needed a job—and that Three Rivers wasn't big enough to supply one.

She pushed the sadness and descending gloom away as she reached for his hand. If this was the last day she could enjoy her time with him, she didn't want to waste it thinking about a future she couldn't predict.

Reese barely made it through his front door after Carly dropped him off. He'd enjoyed the day with her—more than he wanted to admit. Holding her hand as they wandered the streets of Wellington, sneaking between two buildings to kiss her so completely he could barely stand afterward, and then listening to her sing along with the country songs on the two-hour ride home had carved a place inside his heart. A place inside his heart he thought had gone cold.

He put up the footrest on his armchair and closed his eyes, the sweet smell of her perfume still teasing his nose. A smile stole across his face as sleep claimed him.

He woke with a start, the lamp in the living room still burning brightly. Darkness sat beyond the window and the cell phone on his lap vibrated as a text message came in.

*Had a great time today,* Carly said.

Almost midnight, but Reese typed out a response. *Me too. Why are you still up?*

*Took a long nap,* came in as his stomach growled. *Woke up a while ago and can't fall back asleep.*

He didn't want to tell her he'd zonked out the moment he'd stepped through the door and maybe wouldn't have woken for a few more hours if she hadn't texted.

*How are you feeling?* she asked. *Why are you up?*

Annoyance sang through him as he put his footrest down and steadied himself on his feet. He didn't want Carly to act like his mother. Didn't want her worrying about him, or if he was tired after a few hours of walking, or why he was up too late. Didn't want to feel weak around her.

*Midnight snack,* he typed as he put a frozen burrito in the microwave. It wasn't entirely a lie. He was starving, and it was midnight, and burritos could be counted as snacks. Once the microwave beeped, he slathered sour cream on the burrito and sat at the counter as his annoyance faded.

He and Carly texted for a while longer. He puttered around the house before finally heading to bed a couple hours later. Reese had a hard time falling asleep because of his nap, and his thoughts circled the two grants he hadn't sent in yet. He always waited until the more substantial funding was in place, but now he wondered if he should've put Carly's proposed position on every grant and sent them all in at the same time.

*Not much you can do about it now,* he told himself, but as dawn arrived and he readied himself for work, a sense of disquiet gnawed at his gut. At least it was Friday and if he could make it through the day, he could spend another weekend with Carly.

He missed carpooling out to the ranch with her. Missed

eating lunch with her. Missed having her right down the hall, where he could go hear her voice anytime he wanted to.

By lunchtime, the walls of the reception area pressed ever closer. He made his way out to the barn, but Pete had all his boys with the horses in the indoor arena. Reese used to help with the exercising of the therapy horses on the second Friday of the month, but he hadn't done it since his injury in April.

He wandered down the aisle anyway, the oppressive July heat more steamy inside the barn. He kept walking once free of the barn, past the arena where he'd been injured, and out into the open range.

A breeze played with the tall grasses and threatened to steal his hat with one good gust. He pressed one palm against the top of his head and looked into the distance. The sounds of the ranch got swallowed in the whispering of the wind, and a sense of extreme loneliness stole through Reese.

He felt as solid and dependable as the range. It never wavered, never changed. But inside, he felt as unpredictable and unsettled as the weather. Clouds could roll in, soak the ranch and everything on it, hail and leave dents the size of softballs in the tin roofs. He'd seen such devastation during his time in Three Rivers, watched the townspeople come together and help each other, witnessed the tight-knit community whenever someone had a problem, personal or collectively.

"I can't leave Three Rivers," he murmured to himself. He'd been thinking about following Carly wherever she needed to go. He was a good receptionist, though the thought of actually calling himself that and interviewing for other jobs made him queasy.

He watched as a couple of cowboys came in from the range, probably from checking the herd or attending to the bulls. He recognized the black stallion Ethan rode, and Reese's insides squeezed. He'd never talked to Ethan about asking Carly out, though he hadn't really had the opportunity. Ethan was the general controller on the ranch now that Tom Lovell had gone back to Montana.

With the thought of Tom, Reese turned away from the range. He couldn't leave Three Rivers. His family was here. His family that included Pete and Chelsea, and Squire and Kelly, and the horses he loved.

As he re-entered the horse barn, he found Ethan unsaddling his horse while another man lingered nearby. Neither of them spoke, and Reese suspected he'd interrupted a private conversation.

"Hey," he said to him, glancing at the other man. Tall, and dark, and obviously strong, the man flashed him an award-winning smile. Reese had the distinct impression he'd met the man before. "I'm Reese Sanders."

"Tanner Wolf." The man held his horse's reins with one hand and extended his other to shake Reese's. "Came to recruit Ethan to the rodeo circuit."

Sudden recognition bolted through Reese. "Oh, I've seen you on TV. Bull riding, right?"

Tanner gave him that mega-watt grin again, and Reese wished he'd turn it down a notch. There weren't any reporters or cameras out here. "That's right. See." He slugged Ethan. "Everyone will recognize you once you start competing."

Ethan grunted, met Reese's eye, and glanced back to his horse. Something passed between them in that brief moment, but Reese couldn't be sure what it was. He could tell, though, that Ethan wasn't thrilled about joining the rodeo circuit.

"Do you ride bulls, Ethan?" he asked. "I didn't know that about you."

"In the past," he said, enunciating the word *past*. "I have a good job here, Tanner. I'm not joining the rodeo circuit."

"You can make ten times what you make here in one season," the rodeo star argued. "Just one season, Ethan. Just think about it."

"Fine," Ethan said. "I'll think about it." He snatched the reins from Tanner's fingers, which elicited a chuckle from the other man.

"Not sure why he likes horses more then bulls," Tanner said. "But I promised him lunch if he let me come out here this morning." He glanced around the barn and when he looked back at Reese, he seemed like he'd smelled something rotten. "It's quaint. Cute."

"It's a horse barn," Reese said. "It ain't cute." He started to move away. "Well, I have to go grab some lunch."

"Be right in," Ethan said, and as Reese walked away, he hoped Tanner wouldn't be joining them. Sure enough, ten minutes later, Ethan—and only Ethan—entered the Ackerman's kitchen. Kelly had left out barbeque pork, buns, and coleslaw, and Reese had helped himself. Ethan did too, and sat at the table with Reese.

"I thought Tanner said he was gonna take you to lunch." Reese picked up his sweet tea and took a drink.

Ethan glared as he bit into his pork sandwich. After chewing and swallowing he said, "I can't leave the ranch and go to lunch. Guys like Tanner don't understand that."

Reese nodded, that strange understanding passing between him and Ethan again. "So no rodeo for you?"

Ethan shrugged. "I don't know. I'm...." He focused out the window, his lunch seemingly forgotten. "There's not much here for me besides horses and ranching. Which I love," he added quickly, meeting Reese's eye again. "It's just...."

"You're alone," Reese supplied, finally getting it. He'd heard stories about Ethan asking out Kelly when she first started. How he'd put his head down after that and became the hardest working cowhand at Three Rivers.

But he'd asked Carly out only a few weeks ago.

"I'm alone," Ethan confirmed. "Maybe if I got off the ranch every once in a while, I could meet someone. Someone who isn't already dating someone else." He gave Reese a pointed look. "I didn't know, Sergeant. I wouldn't have asked Carly out if I had."

Reese nodded again, not sure what to say. He'd never spent a lot of time with Ethan, but he sounded sincere enough. Ethan exhaled harshly. "So I don't know. I've dated a few women in town, but they're not interested in ranching, and well, it's a way of life, you know?"

Oh, how Reese knew. His own insecurities about Carly roared forward, staining his dreams of a perfect future with her. He knew for certain he wouldn't be leaving Three Rivers, and that she probably would. She didn't like cowboys—had even told him that once. And she hated small towns.

As he finished eating, the volatile thoughts turned quiet as he realized he was in love with Carly. He'd gone and fallen in love with a woman who didn't like cowboys or small towns.

*You're such a fool*, he told himself as he got up and put his paper plate in the garbage can. He waved to Ethan as he left the kitchen, suddenly needing to be alone. He went down the steps as fast as his injured legs would allow him and ducked around the side of the house, his lungs heaving for oxygen.

Panic poured through him, and he doubled over to try to get control. His mind spun, but at the bullseye of the storm whipping through him sat the thought: *Carly never was going to stay in Three Rivers.*

He hated that the thought never changed, never dulled, never quieted. Even after he regained control, after the panic ebbed into silence, after he'd resumed his position behind the counter at Courage Reins, that one, horrible thought remained.

## 16

Carly spent the morning looking for jobs within a two hundred mile radius of Three Rivers. She figured that would give her the chance to work during the week and still be able to see Reese on weekends.

The situation had her stomach in knots, but she couldn't do much to change it. Three Rivers didn't have any viable job openings. And unless she wanted to switch careers and start at the bottom of the totem pole at the bank, or ring up groceries, or take tickets at the botanical gardens, she didn't have many options.

Just after lunch, she slammed her laptop closed and stretched her back. She'd found a dozen positions she could apply for, but her energy for the job hunt had waned. She grabbed her keys and jumped in her car. What she needed was a quick pick-me-up, and because Three Rivers was so small, she knew exactly where to get it.

Betty Sue's Pancake House served more than breakfast, and by the time Carly had her ice cream sundae in front of her, she felt a second wind coming on.

"Mind if I join you?" a woman asked.

Carly glanced up and grinned at Andy. "Of course not. Sit, sit."

Andy slid into the booth across from her, a sigh escaping as she did.

"Rough day?"

"Rough week," Andy said. "Though I'm not complaining. The Fourth of July is just a busy week. Lots of family in town, some tourists for the rodeo, that kind of thing." She ordered a tall sweet tea from the waitress. "And whatever that is. I'll take one too." She focused on Carly again. "And tomorrow's Saturday, which will be crazy. I had to get out of the store for a few minutes."

"Well, I'm glad you're here." Carly took another bite of her ice cream and smiled, though her lips felt too stretched. She hadn't realized Three Rivers hosted a rodeo. But surely it wasn't big enough to attract the stars like Tanner.

"You're not working today?" Andy asked as the waitress set down her tea.

Carly pulled herself from her past, from memories of Tanner. "I lost my job." She waved her spoon like the reason why would be hanging in the air and she could gather it. "You know, because I was Reese's care coordinator."

Andy's face fell. "Oh, that's too bad. I'm sorry, honey. But you and Reese? You're still...?"

"Yeah, I mean, I guess." Carly suddenly wished the other woman hadn't sat down. She didn't truly know her, but she thought maybe she'd like to. Maybe if she had friends in Three Rivers, working at the bank might not be so bad. Maybe she just needed more than one reason to stay in town.

*But Reese should be the* only *reason I need*, she thought, tears pricking her eyes. She blinked the emotion back, unwilling to let Andy see it. She did anyway, and she put one hand over Carly's. "I'm sure it'll work out, right?"

Carly nodded, her voice too tight to speak. She did believe things would work out the way they were supposed to. She'd lived through hard things before, and God always seemed to put her where she needed to be, when she needed to be there. Sometimes, though, it was hard to take those steps of faith with so many unknowns surrounding her.

"If I could find someone to make me choke up, I'd be happy." Andy added a giggle to her statement, but Carly heard the genuine hurt behind it.

"I can help with that, sweetheart."

Carly glanced up at the same time as Andy. A choke tore through her throat, but it wasn't the emotional, *I-might-be-in-love* kind of choke that rendered a woman speechless. More like that *get-me-out-of-here-fast* kind.

The man standing at the head of their table grinned at Andy, holding her gaze for several long seconds before he looked at Carly. His grin fell off his face, and he stumbled back a step.

"Carly?"

Words didn't fail her this time. "What are you doing here, Tanner?" The ice cream seemed to have numbed her insides, but her blood felt like fire in her veins. The warring sensations clouded her head. At least he seemed as mortified to see her as she was to see him.

"Came to see a friend," he mumbled, unable to meet her eye for more than a moment. He tipped his hat to Andy. "Ma'am." He scrambled away, his usual swagger gone. Carly almost laughed that she'd affected him so strongly.

"You know him?" Andy asked, breaking through the ice and fire inside Carly.

"Ex-boyfriend," Carly said, picking up her spoon again. But her appetite had fled with Tanner's appearance. How long would he be in town? Who did he know in Three Rivers? Or had that been a lie?

"He dumped me for the rodeo," she said. "He's in love with himself. No room for anyone else."

"Ah." Still, Andy eyed the exit like she might chase him down and give him her number. Carly paid her bill and headed out to her car, careful to check the lot for Tanner before she committed to leaving the restaurant. She wasn't afraid of him; she just didn't want to see him or talk to him again.

With the coast clear, she headed back to her house to resume the task of finding a new job.

A WEEK LATER, HER PHONE RANG BEFORE SHE'D MANAGED TO DRAG herself out of bed. Her days had become a drudgery. Nothing to do, nowhere to go. At least she hadn't seen Tanner again. He seemed to have disappeared as randomly as he'd come.

She'd taken to staying up until she couldn't keep her eyes open, and then sleeping until she couldn't stand to lie in bed anymore. That still left too many hours to try to fill with exercise, and keeping her quaint house clean, and searching for a job. She'd considered getting a puppy—anything to occupy her time.

She thumbed on the phone when she didn't recognize the number. "Hello?"

"Miss Watters?"

"Yes."

"This is Sam Howard at Eleanor Roosevelt Academy. I received your application early this week, and I'd love for you to come in for an interview."

With those words, Carly's world changed. She sat up and combed her free fingers through her hair, as though Sam was there in her bedroom and could see the state of such things.

"Sure. When works?" She'd have to look up exactly where Eleanor Roosevelt Academy was, and what that position entailed, because she couldn't remember. She'd applied for dozens and dozens of positions, at hospitals, and schools, and professional offices.

"How about Monday?" the woman suggested. "Ten a.m.?"

"I'll be there," Carly confirmed, a thrill of hope shooting through her. Finally. A job interview. Saturday passed slowly, though she spent most of her time with Reese. She didn't want to tell him about the interview. They hadn't spoken much about her job hunt, because she never had anything to report. He was supportive, and he acted interested—he always asked her at some point about how things were going—but Carly detected something distant in him. Something that hadn't been there before she'd lost her job, something that had come during the adventure around the Panhandle the previous week.

"Anything happening with the job search?" he finally asked as she snuggled into his side after they'd eaten dinner on Sunday night. The man could make a mean steak, and she'd enjoyed too many of his home cooked meals.

He stroked her hair, his heartbeat steady and strong beneath her cheek.

"Yes," she said. "I have an interview with a school in Amarillo tomorrow."

She waited for him to react, for his pulse to speed, but all he said was, "That's good news, beautiful. You'll do great."

Something poisonous snaked through her system. "You're not upset?"

He pulled back, inching her away from him until he could see her face. "Why would I be upset?"

"The job's in *Amarillo*."

A muscle ticked in his jaw, the only sign of his emotions. "We always knew you wouldn't be working in Three Rivers." He ducked his head in that maddening way that concealed his eyes from her. "I hate that you have to work at all. If I had a decent job, we could—" He cut himself off, but Carly's interest spiked. Their conversations about her job had never gone in this direction before.

"We could what?" She ducked her face under the brim of his cowboy hat too, forcing him to look at her.

His eyes searched hers for one, two, three breaths, something frantic in his expression. "We could get married," he finally said, his voice barely more than air. "I could take care of you, and you wouldn't have to work at all."

Her heart happy-danced through her chest. "You want to marry me?"

"I believe that's what people do when they're in love."

She flinched at the words, because she wasn't sure she loved Reese. To hear he loved her sealed a hole in her soul she hadn't known was open. "You love me?"

"I do." The steady, strong, sure way he spoke about how he felt made a smile steal across her face. She kissed him, wanting to feel his love in his touch. He freely gave it, and while she reveled in this new information, in the new emotions swirling through her, she couldn't bring herself to return the sentiment.

She liked Reese. Adored him, even. She might even love him —if the situation with her job wasn't so up in the air. He didn't press her to say it back, and though she wanted to, she couldn't— not yet. Not until she had a more solid foundation to work from.

---

REESE WHISTLED A CHILDHOOD TUNE ON THE WAY TO WORK ON Monday morning, his thoughts far away—in Amarillo. He hoped Carly's interview went well. He wanted her to get a job quickly. He knew that was the only reason keeping them apart. The only reason she hadn't told him she loved him last night. The only reason they couldn't start their life together.

As he sat down at the counter with a stack of client folders to go through for the day, his mind turned to the grants he'd turned in last week. He didn't hold much hope for them, and the stamp he gave one paper smudged a little with his force behind it.

His bad mood worsened when his phone rang with a number he didn't know and it was his new veteran care coordinator, Clay

Evans. Reese insisted he was feeling fine, doing fine, everything was *fine*, and managed to pacify the guy. He didn't need to have his case reviewed again, get asked the same questions, talk about his family, his injuries, his plans for the future.

Truth was, he didn't really want a future without Carly. She'd promised she'd call after her interview, but his phone stayed silent through his solitary lunch. Even a quick trip out to the barn to see Peony didn't settle him the way it used to.

"Hey," Pete said, bringing in Hank from his therapy session. "There you are. Got a new horse comin' in this weekend. Thought you might like to be here, learn how we start training them."

Reese couldn't help grinning, despite the stormy feeling in his chest. "Yeah, sure. Thanks, Boss."

Pete acknowledged him with a wave and headed to Hank's stall to brush him down. Reese watched Pete go, grateful the Lord had led him to his Army friend, to Three Rivers, to Courage Reins.

He closed his eyes and sent a prayer into the rafters. *Please, God, help Carly get this job.*

With a bit of the gloom gone, he headed back to work. He moved from the July heat and into the air conditioning when an idea hit him. He froze, almost like he'd smacked into an invisible pane of glass.

"Stupid," he muttered to himself. "Shouldn't have put her job on an equine grant." He hustled across the lobby and behind the counter, his fingers flying across his laptop. He clicked and deleted, his eyebrows drawn down as he searched for what he needed.

He'd done this before—for Gwen when she needed funding for her treatments. "Shouldn't have done the equine grant," he said again. "But a government one. A *service* grant. Social work...." He continued muttering to himself as he read tiny print on complicated websites.

He clicked link after link, read page after page, sent some sites to the printer.

"Hey, Sergeant."

Reese blinked through the computer-screen haze of his eyes, trying to shake himself out of research mode. Carly stood in front of him, wearing a fitted pencil skirt that fell to her knees and a black-and-white polka dot blouse.

She cocked her head at him, and it reminded him so much of the first time he'd met her. He'd been just as smitten then. "Hey," he finally replied. "You didn't call."

A strange look crossed her face, and if Reese had to guess what it was, he'd say fear mixed with joy.

"You got the job," he said, realization dawning. He had so much to tell her about the research he'd done for the past couple of hours, but he held his tongue.

A smile cracked her face. "I got the job."

A rush of adrenaline poured through him, easing the worry he'd been harboring for hours. "That's great, beautiful." He moved around the counter so he could hug her. With her in his arms, he finally felt complete, whole, like it didn't matter if he limped or had panic attacks or had to rest after an afternoon of walking. She'd never seemed to care about those things, and he didn't either—not anymore.

"I'm moving back to Amarillo," she whispered, her breath tickling his earlobe.

The words took a few seconds to register. He pulled back as his earlier ease seized.

"They want me to start on Monday," she said. "Attend the district trainings and everything." She tucked her hair behind her ear before sliding her hand along his shoulder again. "School starts in a few weeks, and I'll need to do some testing before that."

He struggled to make her words line up into meaning. "That's great," he said, because he wasn't sure how to ask her why she had to move to Amarillo to start next week. "You like the job?"

She ducked her head. "I hope I will." She stepped out of his embrace, but didn't fall back far enough to be out of arm's reach. She fiddled with the top button on his shirt, and he wished she wouldn't. The tiny movement made him want to kiss her, breathe her in deep, and never let her go.

But she was moving back to Amarillo. He couldn't drive there every weekend, not in his old truck. He stared at her, this woman he loved, and gathered his courage close, close, close.

"Why do you have to move back to Amarillo?" he asked.

His words seemed to knock into her, force her back a couple of steps. "I—it takes over an hour to drive from here to there. I have to be to work at seven-thirty."

He took a breath through his nose. "Please don't leave."

"Reese—"

"I found new grants." He turned and hurried around the counter to the printer. He grabbed the papers in his fist. "Not equine therapy grants. Government grants. State funding. Social work aid."

"Reese." She shook her head, a fierce fire entering her expression.

"You'd like working here better than at a school," he tried.

"I'm sure I would," she said, lifting her chin in a defiant gesture. "But there isn't a job here. There is one at a school."

He glanced helplessly at the pages in his hand then back to her, the hole that had been stoppered opening again, wider this time. Wider and wider until he gasped for a breath. "Please don't leave," he managed to say again.

"I have to." She took another step backward. Away. Away from Three Rivers. Away from him. "I can't take a chance on a grant. I'm sorry." Her eyelashes caught the tears as they leaked from her eyes.

He threw the papers down on his desk and stalked around the

counter. He caught her in a strong embrace and kissed her. His rough edges smoothed as she accepted his kiss, and he calmed and slowed himself. "Carly." He leaned his forehead against hers. "I love you. Let's talk this through. Maybe there's another solution."

She gripped him like she loved him. She kissed him like she loved him. Reese didn't know what else to do, what else to say, to keep her.

"You could come to Amarillo," she suggested. Her tears continued to trickle down her cheeks.

"That's not my path, beautiful," he said as gently as he could. "I prayed about it and everything."

"There's nothing between here and Amarillo."

"Just sky."

"I don't want to commute that far every day. And I don't want to only see you on weekends." Her words rushed together. "That's not fair to either of us. And I hate small towns, and I can't—do you really think we could get one of those government grants?" She shook her head and spoke again before he could process what she'd said. "No. It doesn't matter. I can't take a chance on a grant." She stepped away from him again. "I love you, Sergeant Sanders, but I just can't stay here."

She moved toward the door, and her heels clicking against the tile sounded like gunshots. Reese flinched with each one, trying to come up with something to say.

But he couldn't. She walked out, never looking back. Her blonde curls bounced against her back, blew in the wind as she climbed in her purple car, got tossed over her shoulder as she backed out and drove out of the parking lot.

Drove out of his life.

He recycled the words she'd said in his mind.

*I love you, Sergeant Sanders.* He smiled, touched his lips and wondered when he'd get to kiss her again.

Everything seemed to slosh from one extreme to another. Hot and cold. Here and gone. Loved and abandoned.

*I can't take a chance on a grant.* He leaned against the counter as familiar bitterness flooded his body, coated his throat, tainted his mouth. What she really meant was she couldn't take a chance on *him*.

## 17

Carly moved herself back to Amarillo, into a shadier part of town than she'd lived in previously. But she couldn't be choosy on such short notice. At least that's what she kept telling herself as she practically scampered from the moving truck to her apartment door.

She didn't have much, and she managed to get everything in with the help of a couple of neighbors in under an hour. With the door locked firmly behind her, she stared at her silent phone, wishing she could text Reese and let him know she'd arrived safely.

She hadn't spoken to him since Monday, after she'd told him she couldn't stay in Three Rivers. A pang of homesickness radiated through her, making her stomach ache and her head spin. Nothing made sense anymore. Three Rivers *wasn't* her home. She shouldn't feel so nostalgic about a place she'd lived for a few months.

In reality, she knew the feelings belonged to Reese. He had felt like home to her, and the thought of never seeing him again had her in a tailspin.

"You made your choice," she said as she ran her keys down

the tape of the box she'd marked DISHES. She just needed a cup of hot chocolate. While she heated water in a mug and dug through a box for her hot chocolate mix, her heart seemed to shrink impossibly small inside her chest.

Driving away from Three Rivers had been harder than she'd expected. But driving away from Reese felt like a mistake she couldn't undo. She'd texted him a couple of times during the week, asking him if he could come help her move. But he'd said he had to work that weekend. Something about Courage Reins getting a new horse, and him learning different things about the organization.

A sob worked its way up her throat, and even the hot chocolate couldn't force it back. She made it through the night by ordering pizza and keeping the television on loud. Her new neighbors probably hated her, but she couldn't stand the silence, couldn't stand being alone with herself, her thoughts, her decisions.

She wandered the city on Sunday, looking for an escape. By Monday, she felt worn thin, like a wet paper towel holding an elephant. She arrived at work earlier than she needed to be there, and sat in the parking lot for fifteen minutes before Sam showed up.

Carly jumped out of the car and headed into the building with the other woman. They chatted about the weather, about the schedule for the day, about Carly's paperwork she'd need to sign that morning.

Sam walked her down the hall to her little room, and once alone, Carly took a steeling breath. This ten-by-ten room was her life now. She'd work with parents and children here. She could make a difference for the girls at the Eleanor Roosevelt Academy.

*Starting my job. Thinking of you.* She thumbed out the text and stared at it, wondering if she could send it to Reese. Would it hurt him? Or make him smile? She knew Reese, and she knew he'd be angry if she texted now. She *had* made her choice—and all fifteen thousand people in Three Rivers knew it wasn't Reese Sanders.

She deleted the text and got to work setting up her office. Sam had said there was a room down the hall with extra tables and chairs, a desk, some filing cabinets, anything Carly might need to get things set up. Carly had no idea what she needed to be "set up," but she wanted a desk and chair, a couple filing cabinets, a table, and some whiteboard markers. With the help of a couple other faculty members, she had her room ready by lunchtime.

She attended a district meeting in the afternoon and returned to her lonely apartment by dinner. Her days became routine. She ate the same breakfast of a banana and a protein shake. She worked through lunch. Attended meetings. Brought mounds of paperwork back to her office. Pre-testing began, and she ensured the students who qualified for government aid received it.

By September, with school in full swing, Carly decided the job wasn't half-bad. Maybe not what she'd pick for herself in an ideal world. But her two-month severance ended on Friday, and she was grateful to have a way to pay the bills, even if her apartment lacked certain commodities—like reliable hot water.

She could move in two months, once her lease ran out.

She thought of Reese everyday. Typed out a text she didn't send. Prayed for his health, his good fortune, his happiness. As she did, she realized she'd never done that for anyone else. Certainly not for Tanner. Not for her mother, even after her father died.

Carly laid awake after praying for Reese, her love for him as strong as it ever had been. Her pillow caught her tears, and though she hated crying, she thought if ever there were a cry-worthy man, it was Reese.

---

WEEKS LATER, CARLY GLANCED UP AS SOMEONE ENTERED HER

office. She didn't have any appointments that day, having sched-
uled her Friday to catch up on paperwork.

Wade Tenley, the school's assistant principal stood there, his
hands held loosely in his pockets.

"Afternoon, Wade." Carly set down her pen. "What can I do
for you?"

He cleared his throat and shuffled his feet. "Wondering if
you'd like to go to dinner with me tonight."

"Oh." A blush crept into Carly's face. "I'm sorry, Wade. I can't."
She smiled to lessen the sting of her rejection. "I have a
boyfriend. He lives in Three Rivers, and we're—" She cut herself
off. Typing texts she never sent to a man didn't count as a long-
distance relationship. Reese hadn't contacted her either, and a
fresh slice of pain cut through her core with the weeks of silence.

Wade flashed a tight smile. "I see. Okay." He lifted one hand
in a wave as he moved into the hall. "Have a great weekend."

But Carly knew she wouldn't have a great weekend. Because
she only had her television and a pint of Ben & Jerry's for
company.

---

REESE INSTRUCTED KARL LYONS FROM PEONY'S SADDLE. "LIKE
that," he said. "Loosen the grip." He shook his reins to demonstrate how they contained no tension. "The horse can feel your
mood, your energy. You have to be calm all the time."

Calmness was something he'd struggled to achieve these past
several weeks. The storm in his chest never blew itself out, even
while he rode. Either Peony had gotten used to it, or Reese had
become really good at hiding how he really felt.

He guided Karl and Raven around the arena a few times, had
them play pony ball, and set Karl to work taking care of Raven
and feeding her a palm full of sugar cubes. As their session
ended, he noticed the happiness in Karl's previously worn face.

He remembered feeling like that at Courage Reins. When he'd first started coming here for therapy, he'd been more broken than he even knew. Everything was better now—except for his shattered heart. And even the horses hadn't been able to heal that.

He headed back into the lobby to stamp Karl's paperwork and make him another appointment. He texted Brett about the kids' camp, something Pete wouldn't let go of. Reese thought he might be able to get out from behind the desk if he could put together a program for children, and he wanted to pursue it as much as Pete did.

Brett had sent him his outline for riding lessons, but Reese had a few additional questions, namely if special training was required for the horses to work with kids.

The mail sat in a pile on the counter, but Reese ignored it. He'd get to it later, when he wasn't swamped with appointments and reschedulings and new clients and texting Brett and making plans for a new summer program.

Later happened just before he left for the day. He sighed as he pulled the stack of envelopes toward him. Some payments, which he clipped together and stored in the lock box under his desk. Some bills, which he'd pay tomorrow. Some thank you letters he'd need to get to Chelsea so she could answer them, and then decide which to use on the website. He pondered the best way to get them to her without having to speak with her. Ever since Carly left, she and Kelly had taken to trying to get him to talk about his feelings.

"Let your emotions out," they said. Even Pete had encouraged him to ride as a patient more often, and he'd taken over the therapy sessions for a half dozen clients. Reese knew Pete had given him those assignments so he'd get out of the building more often, and he was grateful. He was. He just didn't want to talk about Carly yet. Or maybe ever.

The next to last envelope bore a Texas state seal, and Reese flipped it over. He pulled out a single sheet of white paper and began reading. By the second line, he realized this was a letter about one of the welfare grants he'd submitted. Even after Carly had left, he hadn't been able to let her go. Not without a fight. Not without submitting every grant he could find that might pay her to work at Courage Reins as a licensed social worker.

He closed his eyes, not sure if he wanted to know if they'd gotten the funding or not. She wouldn't leave a job she'd just started. Not for him. She'd made that really clear.

Still, every beat of his heart seemed to say her name. *Car-ly. Car-Car-ly.*

He loved her, though he'd tried to stop.

So he opened his eyes and started the letter again. He forced himself to read slowly, but by the end of the second paragraph, he knew they'd approved the grant. For how much, he hadn't gotten to yet. He and Carly had discussed her salary at length, and he'd applied for the amount they'd talked about.

A quick scan, and every muscle in his body turned soft. They'd gotten it. Every penny. Carly could come back to Three Rivers. They could carpool to Courage Reins every day. He could eat lunch with her, hold her hand on the way home, kiss her goodnight.

Fear threaded through him. He couldn't stomach another rejection from Carly. He'd barely survived the past two months. In fact, he still felt like he hadn't quite found his stride post-Carly.

Pete appeared at Reese's side. "Good session with Karl?"

"Yeah," Reese said, flipping the letter over so the lieutenant couldn't see it. "He's doing horse-care with Raven. He'll be in when he's finished."

"Doctor Parchman is ready for 'im." Pete took off his cowboy hat and ran his hand over his shaved hair.

"Great." Reese usually didn't mind Pete's afternoon visits. He'd been popping over a lot since Carly had left. Reese had appreciated it, but right now, while he contemplated possibilities for persuading Carly to come back to Courage Reins, he didn't.

Pete started grabbing at the stacks of ripped open envelopes. Reese let him, because he always had. But the letter got swept up with the garbage, and Reese reached for it. "That's not trash."

There must've been something in his voice that alerted Pete, because he separated the letter from the trash but didn't just set it back on the counter like he normally would've. "What is it?"

"Nothing," Reese mumbled, but Pete was already scanning the front.

"This is a job for Carly."

"I know what it is." Reese met his friend's eye. "I read it."

"You didn't want me to read it."

"More like I don't need your wife knowing." Reese cocked one eyebrow and smiled. Pete threw his head back and laughed.

"Yeah, she can be a little meddlesome. But she just wants you to be happy."

"I'm—"

"Do *not* tell me you're happy." Pete frowned, going from carefree to careful in a split second. "Because anyone with one eye can see you're miserable. Have been since that woman left town."

His melancholy mood had actually started several days before she left town, but Reese pressed the words behind the thin line of his mouth.

"It hurts Chelsea's heart to see you like that," Pete said. "She's just tryin' to help."

"I know." The fight left Reese, leaving an entry for all the misery Pete had mentioned. Reese couldn't deny how he'd been feeling. He knew some of it leaked into his face, showed in his choices. He just hadn't realized how much.

"So what are you goin' to do?" Pete asked.

Reese took the letter and tucked it into his top drawer with his gum and spare change. "Not sure."

"Well, you're gonna tell her, aren't you?"

"Why should I?" Reese asked, feeling a balloon of frustration form in his chest. "She won't come back. She just started a new job, and I don't feel like getting rejected again."

"But—" Pete caught Reese's glare and closed his mouth. "Well, I'll leave it up to you, Sergeant." He turned and strode down the hallway toward the indoor arena. "If it were me," he yelled over his shoulder. "I'd make sure the woman I loved knew how I felt *and* had all the options available to her *before* she made life-changing decisions."

"She's already made the life-changing decision!" Reese called after him, but the door slammed closed halfway through his sentence. He fumed as the echo of his words hung in the air, as he eyed the drawer that contained a future that could allow him and Carly to be together, as he tried to figure out what to do.

His jaw clenched; his fingers fisted; his mind churned.

Seconds felt like bombs as they passed, each one long and loud and liquid. He wrenched open the drawer and pulled out the acceptance letter. Pete was right. Carly should at least know and be able to make an informed decision.

---

REESE DROVE DOWN A BLOCK HE'D BEEN ON TWICE ALREADY. ONCE on the way to her school, where of course he didn't find her. Seven p.m. on a Friday night had only hosted one car in the parking lot. Reese had waited next to it for twenty minutes before a janitor came out. After convincing the guy that he wasn't a stalker, Reese had driven down this road to the address the guy had given him.

But Carly wasn't home either. Reese considered breaking down the front door—one swift kick looked like all it would take —but he controlled his emotions and knocked on the neighbor's door. They claimed she'd gone out with a co-worker, and Reese had growled, "Male or female?" before remembering he didn't know the couple.

They'd assured him it was a female co-worker and that Carly had mentioned going to a quiet, Indian restaurant a couple of blocks away. He scanned the street for the yellow neon sign he'd been told about, or Carly's car.

Relief flooded him when he saw the sign for Tandoori Oven. He parked a ways down the block and got out, his nerves jumping as he thought about striding into that restaurant and talking to Carly. He hadn't seen her in so long, and though he'd practiced what to say on the drive here, his words now fled.

Still, his insane courage had brought him this far, and he prayed that it would take him a little further. *Two minutes*, he told himself as he neared the entrance. *This will only be hard for two more minutes.*

Twangy sitar music met his ears, and the smell of curry assaulted his nose, and he caught sight of Carly in the first few heartbeats upon entering. She sat with her back to him, her glorious golden curls cascading over her shoulders.

The woman she ate with wore a dark, short haircut and noticed Reese as he wove through the tables to their position against the back wall. She flicked her eyes toward him and lifted her chin slightly, making Carly turn.

Her eyes met his, and even through the dim lamplight, he got lost in the depths of their blueness. He took a deep breath, expecting to find the floral scent of her perfume. The tether that had sprung to life all those months ago had been broken, shattered. But it hadn't died.

Time shuddered, slowed, stopped altogether. He reached for her, but his hand barely left his side. She started to stand, but it looked like it took great effort.

Finally, the thread between them connected and life rushed into the scene again. Reese grinned and tapped his cowboy hat.

"Ladies. I'm real sorry to interrupt, but I just need to talk to Miss Carly for two minutes."

"Take your time," the other woman said, leaning back in her chair.

Carly stood, invading Reese's personal space in less time than it took to inhale. She swept her gaze from his boots to his hat. "Reese, what are you—?"

He slid his fingers up her arm, cupped her shoulder, and drew her into a kiss, effectively erasing her question. A skittering wave of desire moved through his bloodstream when she melted into his embrace and deepened the kiss.

## 18

Carly spilled into the street, a giggle in her throat and Reese's hand in hers. She'd need to call Sam later and explain who the handsome cowboy was that had entered the restaurant and turned her world back to normal.

"I can't believe we got asked to leave," she said, breathless in the autumn evening.

"I can." He snaked his hands around her waist again. "You were kissin' me pretty dang well." He touched his lips to hers for only a moment, barely long enough to even call it a kiss. "I miss you so much."

The tenderness in his voice pulled every string in Carly's heart. "I shouldn't have left Three Rivers." She tucked her face into the warmth of his neck and took a deep breath. He smelled like spicy aftershave and horses and fresh cotton, and she committed his scent to memory so she could have it with her always.

"Well, that's why I came." He stepped down the sidewalk, taking her lazily with him. "I was thinkin' you might want to come back."

All the joy of her reunion with him got sucked away with

those words. She'd wanted to tell him a dozen times how much she wished she hadn't moved. In fact, she had typed out those texts. She'd just never sent them. She'd also told him about her frustrations at work, how she was still pushing paper, but this time they bore the names of children instead of veterans.

Helping kids should've felt noble, a calling even. But Carly missed her veterans, the adults she could reason with, relate to, and become friends with.

He stopped next to his truck and opened the passenger door. "I have something for you."

For two insane heartbeats, she thought he'd drop to one knee and propose. She had no idea what to do or say if he did that. But then he handed her a piece of folded paper and stepped back.

"What's this?" She ran her fingertip along one crease.

"Read it."

Tossing him a suspicious look, she opened the paper and read it. With each sentence, her throat grew drier and her hands sweatier. "Is this real?" She lifted her eyes to his, so much hope parading through her she could take over for Macy's this Thanksgiving.

"It's real."

"The state of Texas is going to grant Courage Reins enough money for the salary of a licensed, non-clinical social worker." She read from the paper on the last part. "For real?"

"We already have a psychologist," he said. "But I made it sound very necessary to have someone like you on-staff so we could meet the welfare, health care, and personal needs of our clients." He grinned and pushed his cowboy hat lower on his head. "The state of Texas agreed with me."

She could go back. Go back to Three Rivers. Go back to Courage Reins. Go back to Reese.

"I have a job here," she said, her factual words puncturing the balloon that had been growing in her heart. "I don't—"

"Quit," he said, meeting her gaze with steadiness in his. "That school will survive without you." He stepped back into her personal space, too close to be casual. "I can't survive another day without you. I'm dying in the worst possible way." His husky voice brought tears to her eyes.

His kiss reminded her of all she'd left behind in Three Rivers. All she didn't have here in Amarillo. What she could go home to every night if she quit her job at the academy.

"I'll let you think about it," Reese said, withdrawing his strong arms from her and giving her more than enough space. "You have my number if you need it." He limped toward the back of the truck, where he paused next to the bumper. "I just thought you'd want all the pieces so you can make an informed decision."

She glanced at the letter again. When she looked toward the bumper, he'd moved. His truck door slammed and the engine started. Brake lights painted the dusky darkness red, and then he pulled into the street, leaving her on the sidewalk to decide what to do.

---

"How is this a decision at all?" Sam asked, leaning forward at the table Carly had vacated just ten minutes earlier. "Did you see that man?" She licked her lips and purred. "He was gorgeous. And he drove all the way here just to kiss you. And Carly." She folded her arms and leaned back. "You're in love with him."

Carly couldn't deny any of it. "I just started at Eleanor Roosevelt."

"Yes, and we'll miss you." Sam glanced up as the waiter refilled her water glass. "So, can I expect your two-week notice on my desk on Monday morning?"

Giddiness galloped through Carly. "Yes." She nodded, a goofy smile spreading her lips. "Yes."

Reese woke without knowing where he was. As he studied the unfamiliar darkness surrounding him, he remembered driving to Amarillo, finding Carly, and giving her the letter. And kissing her. Holy smokes, kissing her.

He'd forgotten how good that was, and the ways he missed her multiplied. He stretched and tossed a smile toward the ceiling in his parent's house. His father had welcomed him last night, but his mother had already gone to bed. Reese wasn't looking forward to spending the weekend with them, but he couldn't very well ask for a place to stay for the night and then cut out before dawn.

A moment later, someone knocked on his bedroom door. He startled into a sitting position and noticed the time. Before six. No way his mother was awake yet, and his father wouldn't bother him until he chose to emerge from the bedroom.

"Reese?" a woman half-whispered, half-spoke. "It's—"

"Carly," they said together. Reese struggled to untangle his legs from the blanket, taking precious seconds to get the job done. He crossed the room and opened the door, hardly hoping to find her standing on the other side.

But she *was* standing on the other side. Fully dressed in the same clothes she'd been wearing last night. Her hair looked a bit worse for the wear, but still beautiful.

"What are you doing here?" he hissed. "How did you even know where I was?"

She stepped past him and into the bedroom before a panicked look crossed her face. "Maybe we can talk outside?"

He gestured for her to go first down the hall. He followed, found his dad in the kitchen with a crossword puzzle in front of him, and continued to the front porch.

"I called you last night," she said as she sat next to him on the bench. "But apparently you went to bed early. Your dad answered."

Reese took Carly's hand and kissed her fingers. "So he told you to come at the crack of dawn?"

"No, that was all me. He might have mentioned that he gets up early."

"But I don't."

"I couldn't wait to see you."

He smiled, but he wouldn't look at her. He wanted to bask in the things she said without complicating it with expressions and emotions.

"So you're seein' me."

"I'm giving my two-weeks notice on Monday morning." She extracted a piece of paper from her purse. "Will you send in the acceptance for this grant?"

Reese took the letter, still keeping his gaze trained anywhere but on her face. He thought he might explode from pure happiness. "Gonna move back to Three Rivers?"

"Just need to find a house. Might need to hire a handsome cowboy to do that for me while I finish up here...Do you think Ethan's available to house-hunt?"

Reese growled and then laughed and then leaned over and took Carly into his arms. "I love you, beautiful."

"Love you too, Sergeant."

---

*Three months later:*

Reese cranked the heater in his truck as he pulled into Carly's driveway. December in Texas wasn't exactly tropical, and it had been raining all week. Or at least it felt like it to Reese's hip. It took his truck several minutes to warm up, and he usually drove to Carly's before he even attempted to get the vents to spit out hot air.

He'd arrived several minutes early, so he wasn't surprised

when Carly didn't come skipping down the steps like she usually did when it was his turn to drive out to Courage Reins for work.

The ring box on the seat next to him mocked him—and reminded him why he'd taken such care with his appearance and his timing this morning. He picked up the box and flipped it open to reveal the diamond inside.

He and Carly had been dating for eight months, and their recent conversations had been dancing around marriage.

"It's time," he told himself as he got out of the truck. He marched as well as he could up the walk and to the front door. He knocked, his heart bobbing against the back of his tongue. He wasn't worried she'd say no. He just wasn't sure he was romantic enough for Carly.

The unclicking sound of the lock had him dropping to one knee. He looked up as the door swung open.

"Mornin', beautiful."

Carly stared down at him, her face arranged into an expression of shock. "Reese—"

He held out the open ring box, which silenced her. "I love you, Carly. I want you to be my wife. Will you marry me?"

Tears filled her eyes as she brought both hands to her throat. She volleyed her gaze from the ring to his face, finally keeping her eyes on his.

She nodded, a smile blooming across her face. "Yes."

He'd never known such joy. He thought he had when she'd moved back to Three Rivers. Every time he thought about the wonderful woman who didn't seem to notice his insecurities, his physical limitations, or his flaws. But hearing her accept his proposal was a whole new level of joy he hadn't experienced yet.

He used the doorframe to steady himself as he stood, as she flung her arms around him and pressed a kiss just under his ear. "A million times yes, Sergeant."

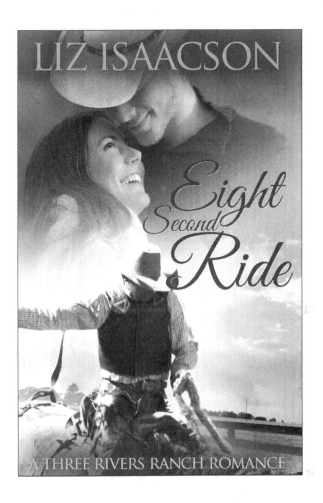

**Eight Second Ride: A Three Rivers Ranch Romance (Book 7):** Ethan Greene loves his work at Three Rivers Ranch, but he can't seem to find the right woman to settle down with. When sassy yet vulnerable Brynn Bowman shows up at the ranch to recruit him back to the rodeo circuit, he takes a different approach with the barrel racing champion. His patience and newfound faith pay off when a friendship--and more--starts with Brynn. But she wants out of the rodeo circuit right when Ethan wants to rejoin. Can they find the path God wants them to take and still stay together?

# SNEAK PEEK! EIGHT SECOND RIDE
## CHAPTER ONE

The clothes Brynn Bowman wore had never weighed so much. Of course, she'd never chosen her saggiest jeans, her oldest cowgirl boots, or a canvas jacket that should've been retired years ago to meet anyone before.

But Tanner Wolf had insisted she make the six-hour drive to the small, Texas town of Three Rivers to pick him up and drive him out to some ranch. Some ranch where some cowhand worked. Some ranch Tanner believed held the key to his calf roping future.

She pulled into the gas station on the northern edge of town, her defenses on high as she coasted to a stop next to Tanner himself. She left the engine idling as she got out and stretched her back, already aware of the murderous winds and cool January temperatures.

Tanner scanned her like she carried a contagious disease. "I told you to wear something nice."

"I heard you," Brynn said as she studied the horizon, where a storm threatened. She pinned him with her most spiteful glare. "I just don't care about what you said."

His dark eyes turned hard as coal, a look he usually wore for someone else. She'd tried a relationship with Tanner a few years back, and that had ended almost before it began. Fun and fast, the broken relationship had left Brynn's fragile ego in pieces.

She'd been picking them up since, going out with a few men here and there, but each date seemed forced, with cowboys who could only talk about one thing: rodeo.

Brynn wanted someone, *anyone*, but a cowboy. Someone who could see she was more than a champion barrel racer. Someone who knew a woman had more to her than a title—if she could even get them to notice she was a woman at all.

Tanner sighed, the fight leaving his expression as he yanked open the passenger door of her truck. "I'm surprised this old beast made it down here."

She'd brought her father's truck, half-hoping it would break down on the Interstate somewhere in Southern Colorado. Then she wouldn't have to be Tanner's errand girl. Why she'd said she'd help him, she wasn't sure.

Oh yes, she was. As she slid into the driver's seat and buckled up, she remembered why she'd driven almost four hundred miles. Whoever lived out at Three Rivers Ranch would be better than Tanner inviting her ex-fiancé to be his calf roping partner. She hadn't backed down in that argument, and her payment was to help Tanner find a suitable heeler who could train in time for the start of the rodeo season in only a few weeks.

"You remember what to say?"

She snorted as she accelerated along the two-lane road. "You practically gave me a script. Say this. Don't say that." She lifted her hand and faced her palm toward him when he opened his mouth to speak. "I got it."

"I could just call Da—"

"Don't you dare," she hissed. "I'll get him to agree. What's this guy's name again?"

"Ethan," Tanner said, his voice on the outer edge of frustration. "And I don't know how you're gonna convince anyone that joinin' the rodeo circuit is a good thing." He reached over and slid his finger down her leg like he could collect a bunch of dust from her faded jeans. "Ethan likes pretty women."

*Great,* she thought. *Another shallow cowboy.* Just what Brynn needed. She'd been raised by a single father who couldn't breathe if he wasn't in a stable, along with two older brothers who worked with horses twenty-four/seven. Becoming a barrel racer had been in her blood, and she couldn't deny that any more than she could force herself to stop breathing.

But after her mama had died a decade ago, Brynn craved the company of someone who didn't wear a cowboy hat, didn't know which brand of boots were best for bull riding, didn't care who currently held the top spot for the Xtreme Bulls Riding Championship.

In her circles, someone like that didn't exist. As Brynn made the turn from highway to dirt road, she considered—again—quitting the rodeo altogether. She wondered what her father would say then.

She pulled into a nice parking lot in front of a newer building and swung her attention to Tanner. "Okay. So where is he?"

Tanner checked his watch like he didn't know what time it was. "He'll be in the horse barn. Invite him to dinner."

Annoyance flashed through Brynn with the speed of a flash flood. She contained it behind a poisonous smile. "You got it, boss."

"Don't call me—" She slammed the truck door, effectively silencing Tanner's words. The horse barn sat across the street to the north, and Brynn strode in that direction. Her pulse thrummed, though she did have Tanner's blasted script memorized.

The sun dipped lower in the sky as she walked, and she cursed winter. At least in Texas, there wasn't two feet of snow on the ground. A few seconds passed before her eyes adjusted to the dim interior of the barn. Someone moved at the far end, and she went that way, reaching her fingers out and petting the multiple horse noses that stretched over the fence to smell her.

The clothes she'd chosen definitely smelled like they belonged on a ranch. The cowboy heard her coming and turned in her direction. He tipped his hat with one hand while he kept a firm grip on the reins of a large black stallion with the other.

"What can I do for you?" he asked, his voice as soft as melting butter. Something vibrated inside her chest. What would her name sound like in his velvety voice?

*He's a cowboy*, she told herself sternly. *And probably about to become a bull rider.* Which, in Brynn's opinion, was ten times worse.

"I'm lookin' for Ethan Greene," she said.

The cowboy paused in his work completely. "You found 'im." He looked her up and down, his bright blue eyes arcing with lightning. His mouth settled into a tight line, his teeth obviously clenched. "Give me two seconds to put Lincoln away."

She wandered down the aisle as he spoke in a low tone and secured the gate on the horse's pen before joining her. In the waning light coming from the barn's entrance, Brynn found broad shoulders, a hint of blond hair under his cowboy hat, and very capable hands on Ethan.

"I'm Brynn, a friend of Tanner Wolf," she started.

"Oh, boy." Ethan stopped and swiped his hat off his head. "He sent out a pretty woman to try to convince me to be a calf roper?"

Warmth flowed through Brynn at his assessment of her looks. She tried to shake it away, tamp it down, but it didn't go far.

"Look," she said, glad her voice didn't sound too sweet, or too emotional, the way she felt. "I don't really care if it's you or someone else who becomes his heeler. It just can't be Da—" She clamped her lips shut. No way she was saying his name. She didn't want to explain about Dave Patton, not to this gorgeous stranger.

He peered at her, something alive and electric in his eyes as he tried to figure out how she might have finished that sentence. She stuck her hands in her pockets and lifted her chin. The end of her braid felt heavy against her chest; her boots squeezed her toes. Why was this man's gaze undoing all her hard-fought years of cowboy resistance? What about him was so magnetic?

No matter what it was, it pulled against her. Pulled, and pulled, and pulled, until she unpocketed her hands and unstuck her voice. "It's a good gig," she said. "Tanner said you're the best rider he's seen in years. So you'll come train in Colorado Springs for a month or so. The pro circuit starts in San Antonio in February. If you can get a sponsor—and Tanner already has his lined up—then your travel and expenses are paid. It's not a bad life. Season ends in December, usually, with the finals in Las Vegas. And the purse is pretty great if you win. Tanner's looking to be a back-to-back champion in team roping." At least she'd stuck mostly to the script. "You can rope?"

Ethan swallowed and she watched the motion of his suntanned throat. "Did Tanner say I could?"

She shrugged. "I didn't get all the details."

A chuckle escaped his lips, drawing her attention there. The temperature in the barn skyrocketed to summer proportions, and Brynn darted her eyes away.

"Right," he drawled. "Because that didn't sound like a sales pitch for the PRCA or anything."

"Oh, so you know about the PRCA?"

His face darkened. "Used to be in it, cowgirl."

The last word lashed her insides, eradicating all previous heat she'd felt toward Ethan. "Fine, whatever. I don't care if you're his partner or not." She finally got her legs to move toward the exit.

He matched her pace easily. "Sure you do. You just said it can be anyone but Da. Who's Da?"

"No one," she snapped.

"Why don't you like the PRCA?"

"Who said I didn't like it?" She stepped from the barn and the wind hit her like a punch to the nose. She flinched, but kept going.

"I have eyes," he said, still at her side.

Oh, she'd almost lost herself in the depth of those eyes. She determinedly didn't look at them again. Instead, she focused on Tanner, on the downward slide of his lips, on the way his shoulders lifted as if to say, *Well, is he coming to dinner?*

Dinner.

The word almost tripped her. "Hey," she said, turning back. "Are you done here on the ranch?"

Ethan looked over her shoulder, which wasn't hard as he stood a good eight inches taller than her. "Why? What'd you have in mind?" He took a step closer, something strange crossed his expression, and he fell back two paces.

"Dinner," she said. "I drove all the way from Colorado Springs today, and I haven't eaten since breakfast." She omitted the fact that her stomach had been rioting against her for days as she prepared for this trip.

Ethan glanced to where Tanner sat waiting in the cab of her truck. "Just me and you?"

Her gut flipped again, but this time because of the possibility of being alone with Ethan. "Sure." She put on her most charming smile, the one she usually reserved for her father and the reporters. "Just me and you."

---

ETHAN DIDN'T THINK HE'D EVER SHOWERED AS FAST AS HE DID after Brynn had said she'd go talk to Tanner and see if he could take her truck back to town so they could ride into Three Rivers together. He'd pointed her in the right direction to find his cabin, and said she could come on in when she was ready.

She wasn't in the cabin when he emerged from the back

bedroom, smelling like leather and his best, spicy cologne. His brain seemed to be battling with itself at a hundred miles an hour.

WHAT ARE YOU DOING?
*Going to dinner.*

YOU LIKE HER.
*I do not. She invited me.*

SHE'S PRETTY.
*So what?*

But Ethan knew he couldn't go falling for another pretty woman. He'd asked out every available girl over the age of twenty-five in Three Rivers. Well, maybe not every single one. He'd gone on a few dates with the same woman several times, but the relationships always fizzled out. Half the time he got down-right rejected when he asked, like Kelly Armstrong and Carly Watters had done.

He didn't want to repeat his past mistakes. He'd been working for a solid year on reinventing himself, thinking that perhaps if he didn't come at women with both guns blazing, he'd have better success.

And yet, old habits never seemed to die. The way he stepped closer to Brynn, all "What'd you have in mind?" made his muscles tighten and his face heat up. He wasn't going to take that approach, not with her.

*Give me the words to say*, he prayed as he moved through his cabin toward the front door. *Help me be the man a woman would actually want.*

The better part of his year had been spent soul-searching,

first as he started going to church with Garth and his wife, Juliette. Then as he realized some of the mistakes he'd made in the past. Then as he started wanting to be the best person he could be. He still wasn't sure who that man was, but he wasn't giving up until he knew.

He pulled open the front door and found Brynn lying in the hammock he'd installed last summer, fast asleep. He analyzed her features while he could. Long, dark hair she'd plaited into a single braid. Dark skin that came from hours in the sun, probably while in a saddle. He recognized the gait of another rider easily enough. Even during his own rodeo days, he knew who the bull riders were, who preferred bronc riders, and who did barrel racing.

He'd pegged her for barrel racing, something that suited her lithe frame and strong spirit really well.

As he stood there contemplating her offer—well, Tanner's offer—Ethan wondered if he could go back to the PRCA. He'd left because his girlfriend at the time didn't want to travel all the time, and she couldn't stand to be home alone while he was on the road.

He realized after he quit, and after Suzy left him, how paranoid she was. How insecure.

But he couldn't force himself to go back—too much pride for that. But this...this could be a way back into the PRCA where he didn't have to explain why he'd left. It had been six years, besides. No one would even recognize him.

At least he hoped not.

Ethan took a deep breath of the fresh, ranch air, and immediately regretted the idea of leaving this place. It had become home, even if he hadn't been able to find anyone to share it with. Even if he'd watched most of his friends find love and settle down, have families.

He still had time. He told himself that on a regular basis, and today was no different.

A door slammed, startling his heart into overdrive and waking Brynn. The hammock rustled, the chain squealed, and she flung her legs over the side.

"Sorry," she said, a delicious blush creeping from under her collar to kiss her cheeks.

Ethan cleared his throat to tame his thoughts. "It's fine. We don't have to go to dinner."

She peered up at him from under long lashes, her mocha eyes capturing his gaze and devouring it whole. "You're not hungry?"

"I'm hungry," he managed to say through a dry throat. "More thirsty, really."

"Hey, Ethan," Garth called from next door. "You wanna—?" He cut off as Brynn unfolded herself from the hammock. "Oh." Garth blinked like he'd never seen a woman before.

"I'm gonna head into town." Ethan hooked a thumb over his shoulder in the direction of Three Rivers. "Should I get that feed while I'm there? Save you the trip."

Garth leaned against his porch railing, his sharp foreman's gaze missing nothing, including the tiny shuffle-step Ethan took to put a teensy bit more distance between him and Brynn. "Sure, why not?"

"Great," Ethan said. "Garth, this is Brynn...." He glanced at her, but she didn't offer him her last name. "A friend of a friend. Brynn, this is my boss, Garth. He's the foreman here at Three Rivers Ranch."

Garth nodded at her, and she man-nodded right back. A flicker of attraction flared to life deep in Ethan's core. He shouldn't be that impressed by her aloof behavior, but he found Brynn...intriguing.

*And beautiful*, the soft part of his brain added.

"Okay, let's go," Ethan said, wanting to grab onto her arm and take her down the steps with him. But she didn't exactly seem like the touchy-feely type. So he clomped down the stairs by himself, satisfied when she followed, caught up to him, and matched her stride to his.

———————

HE MANAGED TO MAKE IT TO TOWN WITHOUT MAKING A FOOL OF himself. Which, for Ethan, meant he didn't ask Brynn out for real or make any passes at her. A balloon filled with accomplishment swelled in his chest as he considered where to go.

"You like burgers?" he asked.

She wrinkled her nose. "Is there anywhere else?"

"You're in Texas." He glanced at her, sure she was joking. Who didn't like a hamburger?

She glared at him. "Anything like Thai? Or a salad bar. I could really use something smothered in ranch dressing right now."

Ethan refrained from rolling his eyes. "You know, you can have them put ranch dressing on a burger." He turned left so he wouldn't have to look at her, and headed for the all-you-can-eat buffet. They'd have rabbit food—and steak.

He pulled into the parking lot, but Brynn protested. "I can't eat here."

Ethan stopped his truck and full-on scanned her like he could find defects just by looking. "Why not?"

"Too many germs." She shuddered.

"Good gravy," he mumbled under his breath. "Why don't you figure out where you want to go?" He didn't mean the words to come out with such an acidic bite, especially because his tone made Brynn's coffee-colored eyes frost over.

"I don't know anywhere here."

"How about I drive around and you tell me when you see something that looks satisfactory?"

He thought she'd like that, but her frown deepened and her fists clenched. "I don't need to be catered to." She reached for the door. "This is fine."

Ethan punched the lock before she could grip the door handle. "This is not fine. You said you didn't like buffets."

"I can cope."

"You don't need to. There's lots of places to eat. Maybe not Thai...."

She flexed her fingers and curled them tighter. Flex, curl. "Why do you care?"

"*You* asked *me* to dinner. I'm just trying to be nice."

"I don't need you to be nice."

Ethan sighed. Even when he tried a different tactic, he couldn't win. "Look," he said. "Let's just start over." He reached for his phone, which he'd tossed on the dashboard when he'd left the ranch. "How about I map some places and you let me know if they sound good?" He didn't wait for her to respond. "Okay, great." He opened his map app, and typed in "nearby restaurants."

"All right, cowgirl, we've got—" He cut off at the sound of a growl coming from her throat. He glanced at her, impressed by how fast she could lock her jaw. "Okay, sorry." He cleared his throat, wishing her anger didn't make him want to call her cowgirl again, see if maybe she'd touch him, even if it was to slug him in the shoulder for being chauvinistic.

"Oh, look, Thai Pan." He tilted the phone toward her. "Never been there. Can't say if it's good or not." He had a hankering that it wouldn't be. Seriously, who came to the Texas Panhandle and wanted to eat Thai food?

He put his truck in gear when she didn't argue and headed toward the western edge of town, where Thai Pan waited. With each passing moment, he wondered how Brynn had roped him into this dinner, into considering going back to the rodeo, into eating food with names he couldn't even pronounce.

Read <u>EIGHT SECOND RIDE</u> now!

# READ MORE BY LIZ ISAACSON

**Love Three Rivers Ranch and want to stay here?** Perfect! <u>Go from ranch to rodeo with EIGHT SECOND RIDE, Book 7 in the Three Rivers Ranch Romance series.</u>

**How did Three Rivers Ranch get started?** <u>Read Heidi and Frank Ackerman's love story from the beginning in THE FIRST LADY OF THREE RIVERS RANCH.</u>

# BOOKS IN THE THREE RIVERS RANCH ROMANCE SERIES:

**Second Chance Ranch: A Three Rivers Ranch Romance (Book 1):** After his deployment, injured and discharged Major Squire Ackerman returns to Three Rivers Ranch, wanting to forgive Kelly for ignoring him a decade ago. He'd like to provide the stable life she needs, but with old wounds opening and a ranch on the brink of financial collapse, it will take patience and faith to make their second chance possible.

**Third Time's the Charm: A Three Rivers Ranch Romance (Book 2):** First Lieutenant Peter Marshall has a truckload of debt and no way to provide for a family, but Chelsea helps him see past all the obstacles, all the scars. With so many unknowns, can Pete and Chelsea develop the love, acceptance, and faith needed to find their happily ever after?

**Fourth and Long: A Three Rivers Ranch Romance (Book 3):** Commander Brett Murphy goes to Three Rivers Ranch to find some rest and relaxation with his Army buddies. Having his ex-wife show up with a seven-year-old she claims is his son is anything but the R&R he craves. Kate needs to make amends, and Brett needs to find forgiveness, but are they too late to find their happily ever after?

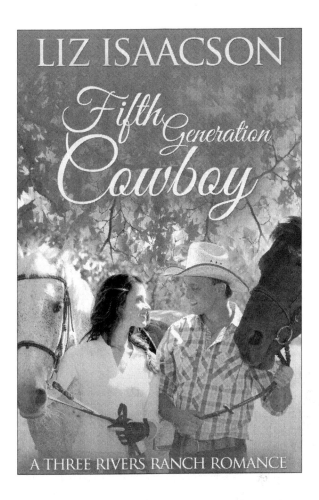

**Fifth Generation Cowboy: A Three Rivers Ranch Romance (Book 4):** Tom Lovell has watched his friends find their true happiness on Three Rivers Ranch, but everywhere he looks, he only sees friends. Rose Reyes has been bringing her daughter out to the ranch for equine therapy for months, but it doesn't seem to be working. Her challenges with Mari are just as frustrating as ever. Could Tom be exactly what Rose needs? Can he remove his friendship blinders and find love with someone who's been right in front of him all this time?

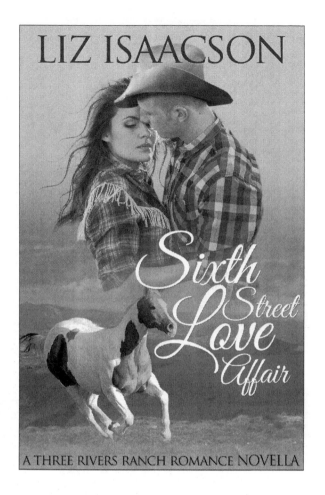

LIZ ISAACSON

*Sixth Street Love Affair*

A THREE RIVERS RANCH ROMANCE NOVELLA

**Sixth Street Love Affair: A Three Rivers Ranch Romance (Book 5):** After losing his wife a few years back, Garth Ahlstrom thinks he's ready for a second chance at love. But Juliette Thompson has a secret that could destroy their budding relationship. Can they find the strength, patience, and faith to make things work?

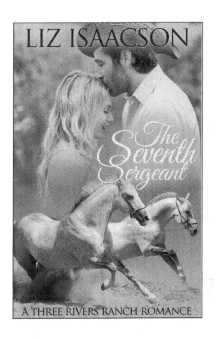

**The Seventh Sergeant: A Three Rivers Ranch Romance (Book 6):** Life has finally started to settle down for Sergeant Reese Sanders after his devastating injury overseas. Discharged from the Army and now with a good job at Courage Reins, he's finally found happiness—until a horrific fall puts him right back where he was years ago: Injured and depressed. Carly Watters, Reese's new veteran care coordinator, dislikes small towns almost as much as she loathes cowboys. But she finds herself faced with both when she gets assigned to Reese's case. Do they have the humility and faith to make their relationship more than professional?

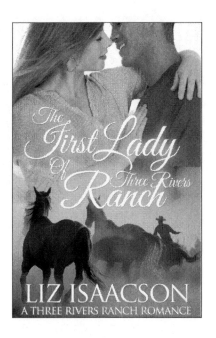

**The First Lady of Three Rivers Ranch: A Three Rivers Ranch Romance (Book 8):** Heidi Duffin has been dreaming about opening her own bakery since she was thirteen years old. She scrimped and saved for years to afford baking and pastry school in San Francisco. And now she only has one year left before she's a certified pastry chef. Frank Ackerman's father has recently retired, and he's taken over the largest cattle ranch in the Texas Panhandle. A horseman through and through, he's also nearing thirty-one and looking for someone to bring love and joy to a homestead that's been dominated by men for a decade. But when he convinces Heidi to come clean the cowboy cabins, she changes all that. But the siren's call of a bakery is still loud in Heidi's ears, even if she's also seeing a future with Frank. Can she rely on her faith in ways she's never had to before or will their relationship end when summer does?

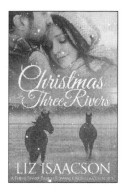

**Christmas in Three Rivers: A Three Rivers Ranch Romance (Book 9):** Isn't Christmas the best time to fall in love? The cowboys of Three Rivers Ranch think so. Join four of them as they journey toward their path to happily ever after in four, all-new novellas in the Amazon #1 Bestselling Three Rivers Ranch Romance series.

THE NINTH INNING: The Christmas season has never felt like such a burden to boutique owner Andrea Larsen. But with Mama gone and the holidays upon her, Andy finds herself wishing she hadn't been so quick to judge her former boyfriend, cowboy Lawrence Collins. Well, Lawrence hasn't forgotten about Andy either, and he devises a plan to get her out to the ranch so they can reconnect. Do they have the faith and humility to patch things up and start a new relationship?

TEN DAYS IN TOWN: Sandy Keller is tired of the dating scene in Three Rivers. Though she owns the pancake house, she's looking for a fresh start, which means an escape from the town where she grew up. When her older brother's best friend, Tad Jorgensen, comes to town for the holidays, it is a balm to his weary soul. A helicopter tour guide who experienced a near-death experience, he's looking to start over too--but in Three Rivers. Can Sandy and Tad navigate their troubles to find the path God wants them to take--and discover true love--in only ten days?

ELEVEN YEAR REUNION: Pastry chef extraordinaire, Grace

Lewis has moved to Three Rivers to help Heidi Ackerman open a bakery in Three Rivers. Grace relishes the idea of starting over in a town where no one knows about her failed cupcakery. She doesn't expect to run into her old high school boyfriend, Jonathan Carver. A carpenter working at Three Rivers Ranch, Jon's in town against his will. But with Grace now on the scene, Jon's thinking life in Three Rivers is suddenly looking up. But with her focus on baking and his disdain for small towns, can they make their eleven year reunion stick?

THE TWELFTH TOWN: Newscaster Taryn Tucker has had enough of life on-screen. She's bounced from town to town before arriving in Three Rivers, completely alone and completely anonymous--just the way she now likes it. She takes a job cleaning at Three Rivers Ranch, hoping for a chance to figure out who she is and where God wants her. When she meets happy-go-lucky cowhand Kenny Stockton, she doesn't expect sparks to fly. Kenny's always been "the best friend" for his female friends, but the pull between him and Taryn can't be denied. Will they have the courage and faith necessary to make their opposite worlds mesh?

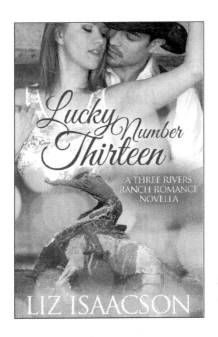

**Lucky Number Thirteen: A Three Rivers Ranch Romance
(Book 10):** Tanner Wolf, a rodeo champion ten times over, is
excited to be riding in Three Rivers for the first time since he left
his philandering ways and found religion. Seeing his old friends
Ethan and Brynn is therapuetic--until a terrible accident lands
him in the hospital. With his rodeo career over, Tanner thinks
maybe he'll stay in town--and it's not just because his nurse,
Summer Hamblin, is the prettiest woman he's ever met. But
Summer's the queen of first dates, and as she looks for a way to
make a relationship with the transient rodeo star work Summer's
not sure she has the fortitude to go on a second date. Can they
find love among the tragedy?

# BOOKS IN THE GOLD VALLEY ROMANCE SERIES:

**Before the Leap: A Gold Valley Romance (Book 1):** Jace Lovell only has one thing left after his fiancé abandons him at the altar: his job at Horseshoe Home Ranch. He throws himself into becoming the best foreman the ranch has ever had—and that includes hiring an interior designer to make the ranch owner's wife happy. Belle Edmunds is back in Gold Valley and she's desperate to build a portfolio that she can use to start her own firm in Montana. She applies for the job at Horseshoe Home, and though Jace and Belle grew up together, they've never seen eye to eye on much more than the sky is blue. Jace isn't anywhere near forgiving his fiancé, and he's not sure he's ready for a new relationship with someone as fiery and beautiful as Belle. Can she employ her patience while he figures out how to forgive so they can find their own brand of happily-ever-after?

**After the Fall: A Gold Valley Romance (Book 2):** Professional snowboarder Sterling Maughan has sequestered himself in his family's cabin in the exclusive mountain community above Gold Valley, Montana after a devastating fall that ended his career. Lost, with no direction and no motivation, the last thing he wants is company. But Norah Watson has other plans for the cabin. Not only does she clean Sterling's cabin, she's a counselor at Silver Creek, a teen rehabilitation center at the base of the mountain that uses horses to aid in the rebuilding of lives, and she brings her girls up to the cabin every twelve weeks. When Sterling finds out there's a job for an at-risk counselor at Silver Creek, he asks Norah to drive him back and forth. He learns to ride horses and use equine therapy to help his boys—and himself. The more time they spend together, the more convinced Norah is to never tell Sterling about her troubled past, let him see her house on the wrong side of the tracks, or meet her mother. But Sterling is interested in all things Norah, and as his body heals, so does his faith. Will Norah be able to trust Sterling so they can have a chance at true love?

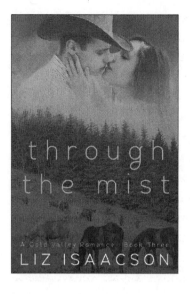

**Through the Mist: A Gold Valley Romance (Book 3):** Landon Edmunds has been a cowboy his whole life. An accident five years ago ended his successful rodeo career, and now he's looking to start a horse ranch of his own, and he's looking outside of Montana. Which would be great if God hadn't brought Megan Palmer back to Gold Valley right when Landon is looking to leave. As the preacher's daughter, Megan isn't that excited to be back in her childhood hometown. Megan and Landon work together well, and as sparks fly, she's sure God brought her back to Gold Valley so she could find her happily ever after. Through serious discussion and prayer, can Landon and Megan find their future together?

Be sure to check out the spinoff series, the Brush Creek Brides romances after you read THROUGH THE MIST. Start with A WEDDING FOR THE WIDOWER.

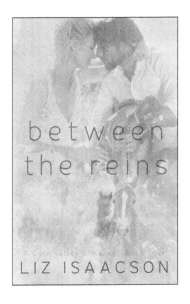

**Between the Reins: A Gold Valley Romance (Book 4):** Twelve years ago, Owen Carr left Gold Valley—and his longtime girlfriend—in favor of a country music career in Nashville. Married and divorced, Natalie teaches ballet at the dance studio in Gold Valley, but she never auditioned for the professional company the way she dreamed of doing. With Owen back, she realizes all the opportunities she missed out on when he left all those years ago —including a future with him. Can they mend broken bridges in order to have a second chance at love?

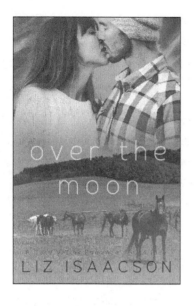

**Over the Moon: A Gold Valley Romance (Book 5):** Holly Gray is back in Gold Valley after her failed engagement five years ago. She just needs her internship hours on the ranch so she can finish her veterinarian degree and return to Vermont. She wasn't planning on rekindling many friendships, and she certainly wasn't planning on running into a familiar face at Horseshoe Home Ranch. But it's not the face she was dreading seeing—it's his twin brother, Caleb Chamberlain. Caleb knows Holly was his twin's fiancé at one point, but he can't deny the sparks between them. Can they navigate a rocky and secret past to find a future together?

Journey to Steeple Ridge Farm with Holly — and fall in love with the cowboys there in the Steeple Ridge Romance series! Start with STARTING OVER AT STEEPLE RIDGE.

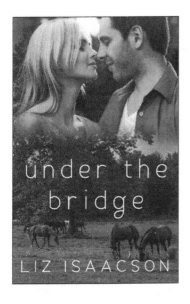

**Under the Bridge: A Gold Valley Romance (Book 6):** Ty Barker has been dancing through the last thirty years of his life--and he's suddenly realized he's alone. River Lee Whitely is back in Gold Valley with her two little girls after a divorce that's left deep scars. She has a job at Silver Creek that requires her to be able to ride a horse, and she nearly tramples Ty at her first lesson. That's just fine by him, because River Lee is the girl Ty has never gotten over. Ty realizes River Lee needs time to settle into her new job, her new home, her new life as a single parent, but going slow has never been his style. But for River Lee, can Ty take the necessary steps to keep her in his life?

**Up on the Housetop: A Gold Valley Romance (Book 7):** Archer Bailey has already lost one job to Emersyn Enders, so he deliberately doesn't tell her about the cowhand job up at Horseshoe Home Ranch. Emery's temporary job is ending, but her obligations to her physically disabled sister aren't. As Archer and Emery work together, its clear that the sparks flying between them aren't all from their friendly competition over a job. Will Emery and Archer be able to navigate the ranch, their close quarters, and their individual circumstances to find love this holiday season?

# BOOKS IN THE BRUSH CREEK BRIDES
# ROMANCE SERIES:

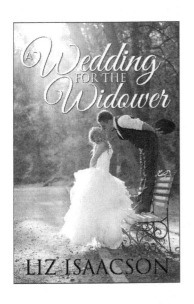

**A Wedding for the Widower: Brush Creek Brides Romance (Book 1):** Former rodeo champion and cowboy Walker Thompson trains horses at Brush Creek Horse Ranch, where he lives a simple life in his cabin with his ten-year-old son. A widower of six years, he's worked with Tess Wagner, a widow who came to Brush Creek to escape the turmoil of her life to give her seven-year-old son a slower pace of life. But Tess's breast cancer is back...

Walker will have to decide if he'd rather spend even a short time with Tess than not have her in his life at all. Tess wants to feel God's love and power, but can she discover and accept God's will in order to find her happy ending?

**A Companion for the Cowboy: Brush Creek Brides Romance (Book 2):** Cowboy and professional roper Justin Jackman has found solitude at Brush Creek Horse Ranch, preferring his time with the animals he trains over dating. With two failed engagements in his past, he's not really interested in getting his heart stomped on again. But when flirty and fun Renee Martin picks him up at a church ice cream bar--on a bet, no less-- he finds himself more than just

a little interested. His Gen-X attitudes are attractive to her; her Millennial behaviors drive him nuts. Can Justin look past their differences and take a chance on another engagement?

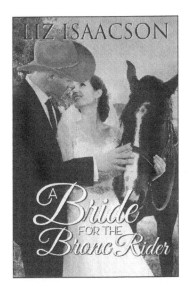

**A Bride for the Bronc Rider: Brush Creek Brides Romance (Book 3):** Ted Caldwell has been a retired bronc rider for years, and he thought he was perfectly happy training horses to buck at Brush Creek Ranch. He was wrong. When he meets April Nox, who comes to the ranch to hide her pregnancy from all her friends back in Jackson Hole, Ted realizes he has a huge family-shaped hole in his life. April is embarrassed, heartbroken, and trying to find her extinguished faith. She's never ridden a horse and wants nothing to do with a cowboy ever again. Can Ted and April create a family of happiness and love from a tragedy?

**A Family for the Farmer: Brush Creek Brides Romance (Book 4):** Blake Gibbons oversees all the agriculture at Brush Creek Horse Ranch, sometimes moonlighting as a general contractor. When he meets Erin Shields, new in town, at her aunt's bakery, he's instantly smitten. Erin moved to Brush Creek after a divorce that left her penniless, homeless, and a single mother of three children under age eight. She's nowhere near ready to start dating again, but the 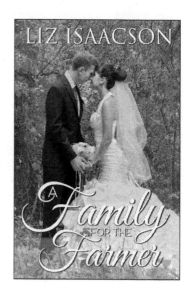 longer Blake hangs around the bakery, the more she starts to like him. Can Blake and Erin find a way to blend their lifestyles and become a family?

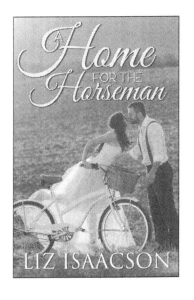

**A Home for the Horseman: Brush Creek Brides Romance (Book 5):** Emmett Graves has always had a positive outlook on life. He adores training horses to become barrel racing champions during the day and cuddling with his cat at night. Fresh off her professional rodeo retirement, Molly Brady comes to Brush Creek Horse Ranch as Emmett's protege. He's not thrilled, and she's allergic to cats. Oh, and she'd like to stay cowboy-free, thank you very much. But Emmett's about as cowboy as they come.... Can Emmett and Molly work together without falling in love?

**A Refuge for the Rancher: Brush Creek Brides Romance (Book 6):** Grant Ford spends his days training cattle—when he's not camped out at the elementary school hoping to catch a glimpse of his ex-girlfriend. When principal Shannon Sharpe confronts him and asks him to stay away from the school, the spark between them is instant and hot. Shannon's expecting a transfer very soon, but she also needs a summer outdoor coordinator—and  Grant fits the bill. Just because he's handsome and everything Shannon's ever wanted in a cowboy husband means nothing. Will Grant and Shannon be able to survive the summer or will the Utah heat be too much for them to handle?

# ABOUT LIZ

Liz Isaacson writes inspirational romance, usually set in Texas, or Montana, or anywhere else horses and cowboys exist. She lives in Utah, where she teaches elementary school, taxis her daughter to dance several times a week, and eats a lot of Ferrero Rocher while writing. Find her on her website at lizisaacson.com.

87291684R00145

Made in the USA
Lexington, KY
22 April 2018